Telling Tales: short story anthology

A Guide for AQA GCSE English Literature (8702)

About the Author

After graduating from Oxford University with a degree in English Language and Literature, and 26 years working for British Airways, I decided to train as a teacher of English. For the next ten years, I taught in the secondary state sector in a multi-cultural and socio-economically diverse area west of London. On my retirement in 2016, I was second in the English department, co-ordinator of the A Level English Literature curriculum and Lead Year 13 tutor, co-ordinating university entrance applications. I am also an Examiner for AQA GCSE English Literature.

I have written three further guides for students of English Literature: *"Poems Past and Present"* covering the poetry anthology specified by the AQA for GCSE; *"Victorian Verse"* and *"Poems of the Decade"*, which cover selections in the Edexcel AS/A level English Literature syllabus.

Contents

About this Guide 1

An Introduction to the Short Story 7

Chemistry – Graham Swift 15

Odour of Chrysanthemums – D. H. Lawrence 25

My Polish Teacher's Tie – Helen Dunmore 35

Korea – John McGahern 45

A Family Supper – Kazuo Ishiguro 53

Invisible Mass of the Back Row – Claudette Williams 63

The Darkness Out There – Penelope Lively 71

About this Guide

The Guide has been written primarily for students of GCSE English Literature as specified by AQA in the post-2015 syllabus (8702). It addresses specifically the requirement **to study one from a choice of set texts, which includes post-1914 prose fiction and that students should study the whole text.** These requirements are assessed in *Paper 2 (Modern Texts and Poetry), Section A: Modern Texts* of the examination. The Guide covers all the short stories in the anthology *Telling Tales*.

The Guide aims to address Assessment Objectives AO1, AO2, AO3 for the examination of this component, namely:

AO1: Read, understand and respond to texts. Students should be able to:
- maintain a critical style and develop an informed personal response
- use textual references, including quotations, to support and illustrate interpretations.

NOTE: There is no requirement to compare texts.

AO2: Analyse the language, form and structure used by a writer to create meanings and effects, using relevant subject terminology where appropriate.

AO3: Show understanding of the relationships between texts and the contexts in which they were written.

AO4: Use a range of vocabulary and sentence structures for clarity, purpose and effect, with accurate spelling and punctuation.

AO4 is assessed in Section A, but is not addressed in this Guide.

The examination requires the student to write an essay in response to a question, drawing on their knowledge of TWO of the stories in the anthology. One text will be named in the question, the other is chosen by the student. **There is no requirement to compare the two stories.** However, in order to assist in the choice of the second text, this guide draws attention to links and connections between the short stories which may be relevant and useful. These links may be thematic or structural.

The stories are explored individually. The format of each exploration is similar:

- An explanation of key features of the story that require **contextual knowledge**, or illustration, and the relationship between the text and its context.
- A summary of the **plot** and notes on **genre, plot structure** and **chronology**.
- A note on **narrative perspective** and **narrative voice**
- An exploration of how **setting** is created and used
- An analysis of c**haracterisation**
- Notes on how **symbolism and imagery** are used
- Exploration of the **key themes**, with a note on possible connections and links to other stories in the anthology.

A note on "relevant subject terminology" (AO2)

This means the use of the *semantic field* of literary criticism – or "jargon". Criticism has a language to describe the features peculiar to the study of literature, just as football has words to describe manoeuvres and equipment – "*penalty*", "*off-side*", "*wing*", "*long cross*", "*throw-in*". To be able to critique literature, you need to know this language and use it correctly. Throughout this guide, literary terminology has been *italicised*, indicating that these words need to become part of your vocabulary when discussing the texts and writing essays. For illustration, here are some very basic literary terms that are often carelessly used and will lose you marks in the exams if you do not apply them correctly.

Text – is the printed words. The *whole text* is all the words that are identified, usually by a *title*, as belonging together as an integrated piece of writing.

A *Book* is a collection of printed pages bound together to make a *whole text*. A *book* can be any text – fiction, non-fiction; play, novel; car maintenance manual, encyclopaedia. A *book* is a **physical** entity, like "*DVD*" or "*scroll*", not a creative one.

A *novel* is a particular kind of text – a *genre*. It is characterised by certain creative features, such as being *fictional,* usually *narrative in structure* and with various *characters* who do things, or have things happen to them. It may be *descriptive*, and may contain *dialogue*.

A *novella* is a short novel. Its scope and the number of characters are often (but not always) more limited than in a novel.

A *short story* is a narrative fiction, of variable, but limited length.

A *play* is another *genre*. It is designed to be performed and watched, rather than read. It can be *fictional* or *non-fictional*, or a mixture. It is predominantly made up of *dialogue* between *characters*, although there may be descriptive elements within this *dialogue* and in the *stage directions*.

A *poem* is a particular *genre* which is characterised by the deliberate, and recurring, use of *rhythm* and *rhyme* and/or by a particular attention to *diction*, in the form of *word-choice* and *imagery*. It is opposed to *prose*. However, there are *poetical* prose writers whose language uses the distinctive features of poetry – such as *alliteration*, *rhythm* and *imagery*.

Beyond these simple definitions, there are a host of other literary terms. These terms have been used where they are necessary to describe features of the texts and are defined on the first usage, and subsequently when repeated, depending on how common the usage and the relevance to the poem under discussion.

A note on "create meanings and effects" (AO2)

The main literary components of short stories are **form and structure** comprising *plot, narrative voice, organisation of time (chronology), characterisation, setting and language.* There are very few marks to be gained by simply spotting and correctly naming structural and literary techniques. Comments on techniques **must** be linked to purpose and meaning to gain marks in the higher bands. This principle has been followed in the analyses of the texts.

A note on "relationship between texts and context" (AO3)

There is a requirement to have some knowledge of the biographical, social-economic, political or literary context in which these stories were written **and show how this is reflected in the text.** Understanding of meaning is enriched by knowing relevant autobiographical details, particularly where the subject matter focuses on relationships. Many writers use allusions and references to classical mythology, the Bible, popular culture and general knowledge, without which meaning is obscure and appreciation limited. Relevant contextual information has been given for each story in either the introduction under "**Context**" or in the analyses.

A note on "themes"

The question in the examination for *Paper 2 (Modern Texts and Poetry) Sections A: Modern Texts* will ask for a response to a central concern or idea which may form the focus of the story or be an integral part of its meaning. You will be asked to explore the presentation of this *"theme"* in one named story and one other story of your choice.

These "themes" could include, but not be limited to: an **emotion** – such as love, loss, sorrow, joy; the **evocation of "place"**, as the subject of the story, or as the setting for the story; the treatment of **abstract concepts** such as Time, Power, Death, or Religion; a "**happening**" such as War, Childhood, Marriage; types of **relationships between people,** such as loving, unsatisfactory, jealous, obsessive, changing.

Where a story from the anthology lends itself to suggesting a particular theme, this has been noted and linked to other stories which have similar themes, to help with the choice of the second story. However, these suggestions are illustrative, not exhaustive; one of the skills to be mastered is to know the texts well enough to be able to link them to themes which may not be immediately obvious. Students should spend some time mapping how possible themes are treated in each of the stories. This "treatment" would include the choice of structure (plot, chronology, narrative perspective and voice), characterisation, setting and use of symbolism, imagery and language.

How to use this Guide

The Guide is intended for students who are already familiar with the stories, in that they have at least read them through. It is not a substitute for reading, and re-reading, the originals. As this is a closed book exam, familiarity with the texts is essential, to be able to make close references to the text in response to AO2.

You should read through the section *"Introduction to the Short Story"* as it gives an overview of the main components of the short story *genre*, and makes reference to the short stories that illustrate these features.

You should read the commentaries with a copy of the text alongside. Line numbers have been given to assist. The texts have been quoted in places for illustrative purposes.

Bibliography

AQA have published a guide to *"Teaching Context"* and to *"Assessing"* this component, which are available to teachers.

Telling Tales

An Introduction to the Short Story

What is a "short story"?

A "short story" is a work of (usually) prose fiction, defined by its length. The "short story" *genre* falls between "flash fiction" and the "novella", or short novel, and although the lower limit for length is usually 1000 words, the upper limit is variable. The upper word limit for entries to the Sunday Times Short Story Competition, the richest in the world, is 6000 words, and similar prestigious Awards rarely allow more than 10,000 words.

Many famous novelists have written short stories, such as Ray Bradbury, the science fiction writer, Charles Dickens and Stephen King. There are other writers who specialise in the short story, notably Katherine Mansfield, Roald Dahl (who wrote hundreds for American magazines), and Edgar Allen Poe. All the writers of the short stories in the anthology (with the exception of Claudette Williams) are well known for their novels.

Components of the short story

Short stories have the same components as novels, but in a reduced form. They tend to focus on a single **plot** line, may be set in a single **location** or **setting**, have fewer **characters**, use limited **symbolism** and **imagery** and focus on a single **theme**. However, skilful short story writers can develop intriguing plot-lines which leave the reader wondering "what would happen next?", create characters in whom we take an interest or with whom we can sympathise, use language that conveys vivid descriptions of places, and contain themes that teach us something about our lives, or the lives of others. In this, they differ little from novels.

Plot and Plot Structure

Plot is what happens in the story. It is the series of events that take place, often created by the interaction of characters, within a particular setting. It is the answer to the questions "What happens?", "Where does it happen?", "When does it happen?" and "Why does it happen?" and "To whom does it happen?".

Plot structure is how the sequence of events is arranged. The most common form of *plot structure* can be summarised as:

Exposition: characters and setting are established. This is the "steady state" before the action starts.

Dilemma or conflict: is introduced into the "steady state" and disrupts it.

Rising Action: events take place which cause further disruption, increasing the tension, leading to:

Climax: the point of greatest danger, or tension, where things could go either way

Falling action: events that take place after the climax and lead towards:

Resolution: where the problems or dilemmas are solved or the outcome is known. Resolution leads to a new "steady state", but one which is altered from where the story began.

In traditional stories, the *chronology* (the order of events in time) takes place *linearly*, as in this model. Events are recounted in the time order in which they occur. However, writers often play around with the chronology of events by using flashbacks (*analepsis*) and flash forward (*prolepsis*). This is notable in Swift's "*Chemistry*", where the story is told as a series of incidents remembered by the boy, which are not ordered sequentially in time.

Narrative Perspective and Narrative Voice

The terms **narrative perspective** and **narrative voice** are often used interchangeably, but are different. *Narrative perspective (or point-of-view)* is *"whose eyes are we looking through?"* as the story unfolds. This is part of the structure of the text. **Narrative voice** is the *style and tone* of the voice that we "hear" telling the story to us – and hence is strictly part of *language*.

Narrative perspective can be in three modes – *first-person*, *second-person* and *third-person*.

In *first-person narratives*, the writer writes as "I". This is the mode used by autobiographies, both non-fiction and fictionalised. *"Chemistry"*, *"My Polish Teacher's Tie"*, *"Korea"*, *"A Family Supper"*, and *"Invisible Mass of the Back Row"* are all written in the *first person*. Of these, only the last is autobiographical. In the others, the writer has created *a persona* through whom they tell the story.

The use of the *second-person perspective* is unusual in prose fiction. This is where the narrator puts the reader *into* the story, addressing us as *"you"*. *Second person perspective* is most often found in non-fiction, when giving instructions, as in recipe books.

Third-person perspective is the most common form of narrative perspective. The forms *"he"*, *"she"* and *"they"* are used. A *third-person perspective* enables a narrator to reveal information about all the characters and all the events that take place, without restraints. Only *"Odour of Chrysanthemums"* and *"The Darkness Out There"* are written in the third person.

There are commonly three forms of *third-person perspective* – third-person **objective**, third-person **limited** and third-person **omniscient**.

In **third-person objective**, the narrator does not reveal the characters' thoughts or feelings directly to the reader. We have to infer or deduce from action, inter-action, description and dialogue.

In **third-person limited,** the narrator tells the story from the perspective of one or more characters, and he reveals the thoughts and feelings of these characters.

DH Lawrence's short story in the anthology *"Odour of Chrysanthemums"* is written in the *third person*. It starts out as if written in the *third person objective*, but becomes *third person limited* at the point where he reveals Elizabeth's feelings as she waits for her husband. The way these feelings are expressed is close to *free indirect discourse* (see below).

In **third-person omniscient**, the narrator is all-seeing and all-knowing. He can tell the reader the thoughts and feelings of all the characters in the novel, and tell the reader things that none, or only some, of the protagonists in the novel know.

Free indirect discourse (or **style**) uses the *third person*, but slips into the thoughts of the characters as if it were written in *first person*. The style of the narrative voice will change. This is different from a writer reporting a character's thoughts, as if it were direct speech, indicated by quotation marks. There is no indication, other than the shift in the *idiolect*[1], that we are listening to the character's thoughts.

Penelope Lively uses **free indirect discourse** in her story "*The Darkness Out There*". It is written in *third-person limited* (we only know what the main protagonist, the girl Sandra, is thinking or feeling) but at times we hear her thoughts as if she were speaking out loud, using her own *idiolect*.

---

[1] *Idiolect* is the style of speaking that is particular to an individual; the grammar, syntax and vocabulary used by that person.

An **unreliable narrator** is a narrator who appears to be "telling it like it is" but whose perspective or judgement is flawed. Whatever the *narrative perspective* chosen by the writer, you have to make a judgement as to the extent that the narrator is telling the truth – is *reliable* – in order to understand the writer's intent in writing. With an *unreliable narrator*, you need to look for other clues – what other characters say, or how they behave or interact with one another, or at the writer's choice of language in creating the character of the narrator - to determine the "truth".

There is an extent to which the boy in Graham Swift's *"Chemistry"* is unreliable. He is a child watching adult relationships and only partly grasping the dynamics. It is this that leads him to consider maiming Ralph, and leads him to overlook that his Grandfather is dead when he visits him. Swift does this to increase the air of mystery of the story – what can the boy/we the reader, believe?

Narrative voice is the voice that we "hear" telling us the story. The *narrative voice* sets the tone of the writing - objective, humorous, ironic, wistful, angry, didactic, informative, confiding, etc. The narrative voice is made up of the particular use of grammar, syntax, vocabulary, – the elements of *style*. The *narrative voice* also creates the relationship between the writer and the reader. Some writers like to stay anonymous – we never hear directly from them; they never address the reader. Other writers break out of their fictions and use *direct address*, speaking to the reader as if they were giving a speech; they may appeal to the reader as *"you"* or as *"Dear reader..."*. Charles Dickens and Thomas Hardy are prime examples of this **authorial intervention**.

We may hear the *narrative voice* of the writer, or the narrator may be an invented character. This invented narrator is called a *persona*. Writers like to explore other states of being, and imagine what it would be like to experience life from a different perspective. In poetry, if it sounds autobiographical, it probably is

– so the *persona* is likely to be the poet. In prose, it is more difficult to determine whether the writing is autobiographical from the text alone– you would need to have *internal evidence* (evidence in the text) or know something about the biography of the writer. In the anthology, "*Invisible Mass of the Back Row*" is the only strictly autobiographical text (although events in the other stories may be drawn from real-life experiences). The story is told in the re-imagined voice of Claudette Williams as a young girl, using her *idiolect*.

Setting

Setting, or *place*, is the physical background against which the story takes place. Setting is important in many stories for creating a particular mood or tone for the narrative. It can also give an insight into the formative influences on the characters, as in Lawrence's "*Odour of Chrysanthemums*", which is set in a Nottingham mining town and reflects the harsh life led by the miners and their families. Place may also act as a *symbol* or *metaphor* for the theme of the novel, as in Penelope Lively's "*The Darkness Out There*", where the darkness of the wood represents the secret darkness at the heart of the old woman. Setting is often used as *pathetic fallacy* – projecting a character's emotions onto the setting, as if the landscape is in sympathy with them, as in the last paragraph of Swift's "*Chemistry*".

Characterisation

Characters are created in three primary ways: *by what they do, by what they say and how they interact with other characters*. The writer may also tell us about physical appearance, clothing, habits and characteristics which make the character distinct from others. Their inner life, or psychology, is usually further revealed by their function in the story, and/or through imagery – associating the character with objects, or a setting, or other concept. In a *third person narrative*, the writer may make it quite clear what he wants us to think and feel about his characters, by telling us: "*She was a tall woman of imperious mien...*" ("*Odour of Chrysanthemums*").

In a *first-person narration,* the character of the narrator has to be deduced from what the *persona* tells us directly about himself, and what we can work out from his actions, speech and interaction with others, as in Williams's "*invisible Mass...*". Sometimes, as with an *unreliable narrator*, other evidence the writer puts before us is at odds with the *persona's* declared motivation, or attitude, to the events he recounts. The reader has to make a judgement as to where the "truth" lies.

Themes, Symbolism and Imagery

A *theme* is a central concern or idea which may form the focus of the story or be an integral part of its meaning.

The title of the Anthology, "*Telling Tales*" is worth considering. First, the word "*Tales*" suggests fairy-tales, which have a particular structure, language and theme. They often have a central, usually female, adolescent protagonist who is threatened by danger and rescued by a young man. These kinds of fairy-tales are considered to be symbolic of "*coming-of-age*" stories. Many of the tales in this anthology can be described as **"coming-of-age" stories or journeys from innocence to experience**. Penelope Lively, particularly, uses the tropes of fairy-tales to structure her story in "*The Darkness Out There.*"

Second, if you "*tell tales*" you are lying. Some of the narrators in these stories could be said to be "unreliable". They view the world from a narrow perspective, as does Carla in "*My Polish Teacher's Tie*", or are young and innocent and see the world only partially. This could be said of the child in "*Chemistry*", and the young men in "*Korea*" and "*A Family Supper*", who have been unaware of the forces shaping their young lives.

Also, to *"tell tales"* is to reveal secrets, to tell people things that either they did not know or should not know. A number of the short stories explore the difference **appearance and reality** and reveal **things hidden below the surface** of everyday life. This is particularly a theme of *"Korea"*, *"A Family Supper"* and *"The Darkness Out There"*.

Last, the narrators in a number of the stories tell us tales of their lives, or a single, revelatory moment which changed them. They deal with the **search for identity and self,** though language or culture or history.

Writers use s*ymbolism* and *imagery* to add layers of meaning to the plot, to develop characterisation, and to help us understand the key themes. These *symbols* or *images* may be clearly signalled by the writer - as in Ishiguro's use of the fugu fish in *"A Family Supper"* - or more complex and developed, as in the image of the chrysanthemums in *"Odour of Chrysanthemums"* or the boat in *"Chemistry"*. *Symbols* and *imagery* may recur throughout the story, in different guises or forms, underpinning the plot and characters and creating a kind of sub-text that aids understanding of the writer's purpose.

Chemistry – Graham Swift

Context

Graham Swift is an English writer and has won a number of prestigious book awards, including *"Last Orders"* which won the Man-Booker prize in 1996. He started by writing short stories before moving on to novels and this is an early work, published in 1982, before his breakthrough novel *"Waterland"* (1983).

Swift's novels are sometimes put in the genre of *"magical realism"*, a term which he dislikes, but he acknowledges that there are elements of the fantastical, or magical, in his novels, which are otherwise firmly set in the real world. The vividly realised appearance of the ghost of the boy's father in *"Chemistry"* is perhaps an example of this style, as at no point is this apparition described as a dream.

"Chemistry" is based loosely on the story of *"Hamlet"*, the play by Shakespeare. In the play, Hamlet, the young Prince of Denmark, is visited by his father's ghost who tells him that he was murdered, by poisoning, by his brother, the new King of Denmark. Having killed the old King, the new King marries the Queen, Hamlet's mother. Hamlet vows to avenge his father. The play ends with the death of the new King, of Hamlet's mother and Hamlet himself (amongst others). Swift has woven his domestic drama around the essential triangle of *"Hamlet"*. Hamlet is the child; the new King, the usurper of his father's place in the household, is Ralph; Hamlet's mother is the boy's mother. The father-figure of the old King is split between the Grandfather and the boy's own father, who appears as a ghost.

The story explores the nature of **familial relationships**, which are perhaps more complex than in the days of the Grandfather's youth. The death of both the Grandmother and the husband of the daughter leave a relatively young woman with a small child dependent on her father – living in his house and off his income. This was not an uncommon situation in the mid-20th century, when women with children often did not have careers or jobs. Many women lived a long and solitary widowhood on the death of their husbands. The idea of taking a partner has only become acceptable, and normal, perhaps in the past 30 – 40 years and Swift explores the impact of this on a man from an older generation, and a child who is too young to see his mother as an individual and fully empathise with her need for a fulfilling relationship.

Plot and Plot Structure

The story is a **domestic drama** - the drama takes place within the home, rather than in the wider world - but also a **domestic mystery**, as it involves two deaths (of the Grandfather and the Father) and the unresolved mystery of the sinking of the boat. It is also a "**coming-of-age**" story, as we see the boy come to terms with the adult world and his place in it.

The narrator is a ten-year-old boy who, by the age of eight, has lost both a Grandmother (Vera) and a Father (Alec). The death of the Grandmother causes tension between the generations, as the Father and Mother refuse to move in with the Grandfather, who is now living alone. However, the sudden death of the Father in a plane crash leads to the Mother and Son going to live with the Grandfather and forming a close family bond, living apparently "*contentedly*" together (line 67). A particularly enjoyable activity for the Grandfather and son is sailing a boat across the local pond, the boy on one side, Grandfather on the other, while the Mother watches.

However, this harmony is disrupted when the Mother meets a man, Ralph, who quickly moves into the household. This coincides with the sinking of the boat. Tension between the Grandfather and Ralph mount, the old man resenting the intrusion of the newcomer and the Mother torn between loyalty to her Father and her desire for a partner. On an evening full of tension, the Mother finally sides with Ralph, banishing the Grandfather from his own house, to his shed.

The boy comes to be a regular visitor to his Grandfather's shed, where the old man now lives, except for sleeping, when he returns to the house. His Grandfather shows him his chemistry "experiments", identifying various chemical solutions, including a flask of hydrochloric acid and another of prussic acid, a poison. One night, seeing his mother in the embrace of Ralph, the boy decides that he now has the wherewithal to restore the equilibrium between the Grandfather, Mother and son by maiming Ralph *"so Mother would no longer want him."* The night before he decides to do the deed, and steals the hydrochloric acid from the shed while his Grandfather appears to be asleep, but is possibly already dead, his Father appears to him as a ghost, and tells him that it is his Mother who sabotaged the boat.

The boy is awoken the next morning by voices and goes downstairs to see his Grandfather being carried out to an ambulance. He learns later that he committed suicide by drinking the prussic acid.

The story ends with the boy struggling to come to terms with the death and find answers to his questions. He revisits the pond where his boat lies sunk at the bottom. He sees his Grandfather on the other side, his hands still reaching out to catch it.

The story is told in the past tense, but non-linearly. This makes the sequence of events, at times, difficult to piece together. Swift uses these shifts in time-frame to heighten the tension and to delay the resolution of the drama, as well as to develop the central symbol of the boat. The story opens with the boat sinking, just as Ralph arrives on the scene, foreshadowing the tragic outcome; moves forward to the night of the banishment; recaps the circumstances of how they came to be living in the Grandfather's house; moves forward to recall other incidents between Ralph and his Grandfather; brings us back to the evening of the banishment; moves back to a time before Ralph and the construction of the boat; moves forward to the months following the banishment and then proceeds linearly to the death of the Grandfather and the boy's visit to the pond.

Narrative Perspective and Voice

The story is a *first-person narrative* told by an adult looking back on events in his childhood. The narrative *voice* is of the adult throughout – Swift does not use the *idiolect*[2] of a child to tell the story. However, the *perspective* remains predominantly that of the child, the adult mostly refraining from questioning the truthfulness of the child's account. He does this by qualifying the child's account: "*It seemed to me…*"; "*I don't think …*", "*Perhaps…*". At times Swift does use the "benefit of hindsight" to comment on events, as when he speculates on the "*vengeful delight*" of his Grandfather on the death of his son-in law. That there might be another, possibly valid, perspective on the events of the drama that unfolds is given to us in snippets of reported conversation, whose meaning is largely lost on the child. In the opening passage, the Grandfather speaks out loud after the boat sinks, saying: "*You must accept it – you can't get it back – it's the only way*" (line 23). The child takes this to refer to the boat – but the reaction of the mother, "*as if she had seen something appalling*", tells us that she knows the old man is referring to her betrayal (as he sees it) of her dead husband, by taking up with Ralph.

---

[2] *Idiolect* is the particular way of speaking of an individual, made up of grammar, pronunciation and vocabulary.

Setting

The story is set mainly in winter; even though it moves back and forth in time, a chill pervades the whole, reflecting the bleakness of the tale. There are two key settings in the story – the pond on which the boy and his Grandfather sail the boat, and the shed. Each are places important to the memory of the Grandfather and characterise their relationship.

The pond is described as *"circular, exposed"* (line 1), cold and uninviting. It is the ritual the three indulge in, the sending of the boat across the pond from grandson to Grandfather, that brings warmth and life to this bleak environment. They are bound together by familial ties, and can overcome anything together.

The shed is the *"miniature"* (line 119), and spiritual home of the Grandfather, where the boy believes he *"communes"* with his dead wife. It is here that the old man can find comfort and feel less *"alone"*. It is also where the child finds refuge from the confusing relationship between Ralph and his Mother. In detailing the *"flasks, tubes and retort stands"*, the *"single electric lightbulb"*, the *"gas cylinder"* and *"glass fronted cupboard"* (lines 130 – 137) the boy can hang on to something solid and dependable – something *"safe"* which operates by known laws.

Characterisation

Our perceptions of the characters in the story are largely determined by the perceptions of the child. His prejudices, and his act of "balancing" the domestic triangle, dictate the aspects of the characters that are given prominence. This brings ambiguity – how are we supposed to react to Ralph's "intrusion", the Grandfather's stubborn resistance to change and the Mother's weakness in giving in to her new partner? Should we be seeing the old man as selfish, the woman as pragmatic and the child as self-absorbed?

The child is clearly wary of **Ralph**, who "*shouts*" (line 26), and "*pounces*" (line 29) and "*barks*" (line 31) and about whom there is an air of violence. The boy is "*often afraid he might hit me*" (line 80) and he thinks he is capable of "*seizing his Grandfather by the throat*". The boy vehemently refuses Ralph's offering of a new boat, thus asserting his loyalty to his Grandfather and Father (line 30). Ralph's appetites are for both food ("*You see, he liked his food.*" line 98), which he "*gobbled*" (line 199), and the boy's Mother ("*his big, lurching frame almost enveloping her...*" line 185-6). Ralph's relationship to the Mother is smothering, sexually charged and domineering. Not only does he "move in" but he "takes over", upsetting the equilibrium established by the three.

The Mother, who is never named, is seen entirely through the eyes of the child and in relation to the men in her life. She speaks little, her only statement being when she sides with Ralph to banish her father to his shed. She is described as largely passive "*very still and very white*", and helpless ("*What am I to do?*" line 101 and "*trapped and helpless*" line 188).

However, she is the *catalyst*[3] in the plot – it is she that disrupts the "steady state" by introducing Ralph into the triangle. The child believes, up to the moment she banishes the Grandfather, that she will stand firm alongside them: "*now we are going to show our solidarity*" (line 113). The boy has no concept of her inner life or what she wants or needs. The boy's disappointment in her, and feeling of betrayal, is evident by the appearance of the ghost of his Father, who accuses her of sabotaging the boat, which the boy declares he "*believes*" and will "*prove*". (line 215). It is also evident in the actions he picks out after his Grandfather's death: "*this look of relief*" (line 232); saying "*There – isn't that lovely?*" as she throws open the windows of the old man's room,

---

[3] A *catalyst* is something which speeds up a chemical reaction. In literature, it is used to describe the event, or character, that creates the problem or dilemma in the plot.

letting in light and air, but also banishing the old man once again. Her lack of empathy with the child is marked; she effectively silences him after the death, and fails to answer his questions. Particularly disturbing is his unanswered pondering of *"how suicide can be murder"*. We are left wondering how their relationship will develop as he grows older.

Sympathy for **the Grandfather** is created through the boy's worship of him. He is the father that he has lost. The child focuses on his hands as the record of the life he has led (*"knotted, veiny and mottled"*, (line 16) and *"acid-marked"* (line 258), but they are also the safe pair of hands that will keep the child on a steady path: *"reach out, grasp it and set it on its return"* (line 16). The Grandfather can fulfil the boy's emotional needs, he is kind and seen, by the boy, as keeping him and his Mother *"as he might have kept his own wife and son"* (line 69). The boy sees no reason to introduce another into their family unit. Thus, he is prejudiced against Ralph, siding with the old man from the outset.

However, the old man is clearly stubborn; when his wife, Vera, dies, he falls out with his daughter because she will not move her family into his house. He belongs to a generation that believed in marriage for life, and faithfulness after death, and is not sympathetic to his daughter's loneliness, insisting that she be stoical and accept her widowhood: *"You must accept it – you can't get it back – it's the only way"* (line 23). As an adult, the boy wonders if his Grandfather took a *"secret, vengeful delight"* (line 63) in the son-in-law's death. There is defiance in him isolating himself in the shed. Even the boy acknowledges that in the house, he is *"sour and cantankerous."*

We see the old man's age and vulnerability through the boy's eyes as well. He is described as *"weary, ailing"* (line 141) and *"a torpid, captive animal"* (line 191) that slips into his house *"like a stray cat"* (line 203). The Grandfather's intellectualism, his desire to learn through his experiments, is contrasted with Ralph, the creature of appetite, who swills beer while smothering the Mother.

Themes, Symbolism and Imagery

The single-word title *"Chemistry"* is rich in meaning, allowing for the development of a number of themes. First, there is the literal meaning of the science of the *composition, behaviour and properties of matter*, illustrated by the Grandfather's experiments in his shed, with its *"flasks, tubes and retort stands"* (line 132). However, the Grandfather describes chemistry as *"the science of change"*, illustrating this by dissolving *"marble chips in nitric acid"* (lines 130 – 146). Through this, the idea of **changing relationships** or **changing dynamics** within relationships is reinforced, referring to the power struggle that exists between the Grandfather and the duo of his daughter and her new partner. As the old man states: *"People change too, don't they?"* (line 163).

"**Bonds**", in the science of chemistry, are what hold matter together – in this story, the family unit of Grandfather, mother and grandson. **Hereditary ties,** what we inherit from our parents and ancestors down the ages, bind people together. This is explored when the Grandfather points to the example of the element Gold, which remains the same, even if outwardly changed, its essential nature remaining constant. This image is developed by the boy seeing his Grandfather's face as *"some infinite stick of rock"*, in which a repeating image, father to mother to son, is stamped. Also, the boy speculates that he must have had his Grandmother's *"looks"*, as his Mother and Grandfather *"would often gaze curiously at [his] face"* (line 41) and his mother would seek signs of her dead husband in his face, holding her son tight unless he, too, should *"turn into air"* and leave her (line 62). These images reinforce the idea that the Grandfather, his daughter, and his grandson are bound together by indissoluble bonds (lines 167 – 172) and that the new partner, Ralph, is an "outsider".

This idea is also reinforced by the image of the boat sent across the pond between the Grandfather and the grandson, while the mother stands behind, forming an *"invisible cord"* (line 13) between them. The sinking of this boat, soon after Ralph appears on the scene, is symbolic of the threat of the new partner, Ralph, to the fragile domestic triangle (*"the delicate equilibrium"*) that exists between the old man, his daughter and the boy (line 87). When they try to retrieve the boat, all that comes out of the water is "*weeds*" - unwanted, useless, barren, foreshadowing the breakdown of the family unit. The ghost-Father accuses the Mother of the sabotage, as a manifestation of the child's feeling that his Mother has betrayed them and broken these bonds.

Chemistry is also a colloquial term for **the feelings that draw people together**, as the Mother has been drawn to the new partner, bonding with him and, in making that bond, excluding both her son and her father. The child cannot understand, and the Grandfather refuses to recognise, the **woman's sexuality** which is the *catalyst* for the change that occurs. The child describes this newly formed bond as an *"equation"* (line 90) which he constantly balances and rebalances as the dynamic between the foursome shifts. There is also the idea of the child being the *fulcrum* in this balancing act, being in the middle of this changing dynamic.

"Chemistry" is also a *"***coming-of-age story***"*, showing a child's **transition from childhood to adolescence** or from **innocence to experience.** This transition is often triggered by a traumatic event, as a result of which the innocent, largely ignorant of the workings of the adult world, moves to experience, acquiring an understanding of the adult world and their place in it. The boy's reaction to Ralph and his solution to the problem, shows his innocence. The death of his Grandfather, and his mother's relieved reaction to it, causes him to consider **things buried below the surface** and to understand that *"though things change*

they aren't destroyed" (line 253). Even though the boat has sunk below the water, it is still there. Love and Memory endure.

Water imagery is used in a number of the stories to convey the idea of **"hidden depths"**. In *"Chemistry"*, it is the boat sunk beneath the pond; in *"Korea"* it is the eels and fishing in the river; in *"A Family Supper"* the soup hides a potentially lethal fish; in *"The Darkness Out There"*, Mrs Rutter's face is described as a *"creamy smiling pool"* and her voice as *"flowing on"*.

Links

"*Odours of Chrysanthemums"*, *"Korea"* and *"A Family Supper"* are also **domestic dramas** which explore **familial relationships** and reveal **the tensions below the surface** of everyday lives.

"Korea" and *"A Family Supper"* both feature a young, troubled male, or male child, who is coming to terms with an adult world that he has does not fully understand, making them **"coming-of-age"** stories. In *"Invisible Mass of the Back Row"*, Hortense moves from Jamaica to England, and discovers a new sense of **identity**. Sandra, in *"The Darkness Out There"*, also has to re-evaluate her beliefs about how the adult world works as the darkness at the heart of people is revealed to her as she moves from a state of **innocence to experience**.

Both *"Chemistry"* and *"Odour of Chrysanthemums"* explore **female sexuality**. The Mother and Elizabeth are struggling with their sexuality; the Mother gives in to her need for a partner, Elizabeth wonders how she can have made love to someone she barely knew. Sandra, in *"The Darkness Out There"*, is a young girl on the verge of womanhood whose ideas of men and sex is based on childhood fantasies but whose experience in the cottage shows her a future reality.

Odour of Chrysanthemums – D. H. Lawrence

Context

D.H. Lawrence is a towering figure in early 20th-century literature for the boldness of his subject matter. He is notorious for his novel *"Lady Chatterley's Lover"* (1928) which, when first published openly in Britain in 1960, led to an obscenity trial against Penguin Books, as it was sexually explicit and used "four-letter words". Penguin won, which largely removed the threat of censorship from books thereafter. Lawrence's subject matter is autobiographical, reflecting his childhood and youth as the son of a miner in a Nottinghamshire mining town, his deep affection for his mother, who died when he was 25, and his relationships with women, including his wife, Frieda, with whom he lived adulterously for two years (and who had left her husband and three children) before marrying in 1914. Lawrence had spent some time travelling abroad with Frieda and eventually exiled himself from England, in what he described as his *"savage pilgrimage"*, worn down by the rejection and banning of his novels *"The Rainbow"* (1915) and *"Women in Love"* (1916), and the suspicions of the military authorities, as Frieda was German. He spent most of his life thereafter travelling, spending much of his time in America and Mexico.

"Odour of Chrysanthemums" is one of Lawrence's earliest published works, appearing in the literary magazine, the *English Review,* in 1908. It was commissioned by the editor, Ford Maddox Ford, who had been sent some of his poems by Lawrence's friend, and later lover, Jessie Matthews, and he wanted more tales of Nottinghamshire mining life. Even in this early work, Lawrence's uncompromising attitude towards portraying sexual relationships between men and women is evident, as is his acknowledgement and discussion of female sexuality – a subject which was largely

unexplored by writers of the time. It is this frankness that made his novels difficult to publish and subject to censorship.

The story is typical, too, in its portrayal of the details of miners' lives at the turn of the 20th century, which is harsh and uncompromising. There is no glamourizing of their lives; they are impoverished, uneducated, worked long hours underground, had little leisure, and drinking was a way to escape the unrelenting drudgery. Mining was dangerous; in the early years of the century, deaths in Nottinghamshire mines were running at five per month, peaking in 1929 at 64 deaths in the year[4]. Men also died young of diseases, such as *pneumoconiosis,* caused by breathing in coal-dust. On the other hand, Lawrence paid tribute to the stoicism of the miners and their families, their strength in adversity, and their close-knit communities which invests them with a kind of nobility.

Plot and Plot Structure

The story tells of a woman's reaction to the death of her husband in a mining accident. She re-evaluates their life together and concludes that they never really knew each other, even though they were married for years, had two children and were expecting a third.

The story opens with an extended scene setting, describing the mining town, and the train descending into the village, past the cottage where the train driver's daughter, Elizabeth Bates, lives. As she walks from the garden to the yard by the house with her son, John, she picks a sprig of chrysanthemums and absent-mindedly pushes them into the band of her apron. She waits in the yard with her son for the train to arrive, so she can go through the ritual of handing up a cup of tea to her father. In their conversation, the father reveals that he is planning to remarry

---

[4] Alan Beales, Nottinghamshire Post, September 2010

and we learn that his daughter's husband, who is a miner, is a drunk.

The father is late home from the mine and Elizabeth suspects that he is drinking at the pub. While waiting, Elizabeth prepares tea and she and the children sit down to eat. The elder, child, Annie notices the sprig of chrysanthemums in her mother's waistband and is delighted. Elizabeth is relieved that she has not noticed that her mother is pregnant. The tension in the cottage mounts as time drags on and the father does not arrive. Elizabeth tells the anxious children that if their father comes, he will be carried in senseless with drink, like a "*log*", which means there will not be a "*scene*", implying that he is violent when drunk. The mother decides to put the children to bed and go and look for her husband, as her anxiety is now turning to fear.

Reluctant to enter the local pub, Elizabeth asks her neighbours for news, but no-one has seen her husband. Her neighbour agrees to ask around the village, so she can return to the children at home. While she waits for news, her mother-in-law arrives to tell her that there has been an accident at the pit and that she has been sent to warn Elizabeth that the men are bringing her husband home. The mother confirms that Elizabeth is pregnant.

Men arrive carrying the body of Elizabeth's husband, who has been asphyxiated by a rock fall in the pit. As was customary, they lay the body out in the parlour, while Elizabeth goes to soothe the children who have been woken up by the noise of the grandmother's moaning. Elizabeth and her mother-in-law wash and dress the body together. While handling his body, Elizabeth realises the great gulf that lay between them when he was alive, how little they knew each other, and how much greater the gulf is between life and death.

The story is told in the past tense and linearly - the events described happen as they occur. Tension is created by the repeated references to the passing of time; Elizabeth clock-watches as she waits for her husband's return, and as the hour grows later, we see her anger give way to anxiety and finally fear. Lawrence also raises the tension when Elizabeth momentarily loses her self-control and tells the children that her husband will be brought home drunk, like a *"log"* (line 197), *foreshadowing*[5] the end of the story.

Narrative Perspective and Voice

The story begins in *third-person objective*. The *"voice"* we hear is Lawrence's, as he describes in realistic detail the mining town, the voyage of the train, and the miner's cottage. Through much of the time we watch Elizabeth in the cottage, we are only aware of her thoughts and feelings, from her tone of voice (as in *"said the woman bitterly)"*, from her movements or gestures (*"the stern unbending of her head"*), or from her speech, which are precisely detailed. This gives us the sense that Elizabeth is exercising considerable self-control, to protect her children and her self-esteem, but inside is harbouring a seething mass of pent up emotion.

However, as the tension mounts, increasingly the perspective moves to *third-person limited* as Lawrence begins to allow us into Elizabeth's internal world and we begin to see her *perspective* and judgement on the events unfolding: *"his dinner spoiled and wasted"* (line 95); *"her heart burst with anger at their father, who caused all three such distress"* (line 203).

Gradually, the revelation of her thoughts and feelings comes close to *free indirect discourse*, as Lawrence uses Elizabeth's own words, with no indication of the shift between his, and her, *narrative voice*: *"At a quarter to ten there were footsteps. One*

---

[5] *Foreshadowing* is anticipating events further on in the story, The significance of what is said or what happens is only realised when the story has ended.

person!" (line 293) or "how tiresome he would be to nurse!" (line 325).

Much of the story is told through *dialogue* between Elizabeth and the people she encounters as she waits for her husband to return. This *dialogue* is written in the *dialect*[6] of the Nottinghamshire miners, giving it authenticity. It also draws a contrast between Elizabeth and her neighbours, putting her apart from them (see *Characterisation*).

Setting

The setting is part of the *exposition* of the story and strongly realised. The journey of the engine from Selston leads us through the miners' environment to the miner's cottage, where we are introduced to the main interest of the story – Elizabeth. On the way, it passes through a blighted landscape, where nature seems to be struggling to survive: the oak-leaves are *"withered"* (line 8); the birds disappear into the dusk; the fields are *"dreary and forsaken"* (line 11). The light is baleful and hellish, cast by *"flames like red-sores"* and the light is *"stagnant"* (line 13).

This is a man-made landscape in which man is subservient to Coal. The woman whom the train passes is *"insignificantly trapped"* (line 7), and the miners *"passed like shadows"* (line 18). Elizabeth's cottage is *"squat"* below the cinder train tracks, and seems to be under threat from the *"bony vine"* which *"clutches"* at the roof (line 20). The plants in the garden fail to bring cheer; they are *"wintry"*, *"twiggy"*, *"ragged"*. The pink chrysanthemums are described as *"dishevelled"*, hanging on the bushes like dishcloths (lines 21-23). Against this backdrop, the miners seem to hang on to life grimly, finding what little pleasure they can in the public houses. The setting also serves to show the contrast

---

[6] *Dialect* is the speech of people from a particular region, or from a particular socio-economic group, distinguished from Standard English by grammar, syntax, vocabulary and pronunciation.

between Elizabeth and the environment in which she lives (see *Characterisation*).

The second important setting is the interior of the cottage. It is presented as a warm and welcoming contrast to the drear exterior. This is Elizabeth's world, over which she has some control and we learn from the setting much about Elizabeth's character. The emphasis here is on warm light: *"full of firelight"*; *"red coals piled glowing"*; *"cups glinted in the shadows"* (line 87-89). Lawrence contrasts this cosy, orderly interior with the chaotic mess of the cottage of the miner's wife whom she visits to seek her husband, with the repeated use of *"litter"* and the listing of the piles of clothes on the sofa (*"squab"*) and floor, and the mess of used tea-things on the oil-cloth-covered table[7] (line 243). Elizabeth notes that the woman has twelve children, her *"faint disapproval"* giving way to resignation. This is the life to be expected by a miner's wife.

However, as the evening draws on and the husband fails to return, this cheerful warmth and glow gives way to darkness: *"the fire was sinking and the rooms was dark red"* (line 101). The darkness outside is *"uncertain"*, as hope that the man will return begins to die, ushering in the fearful thought that he might never return.

Characterisation

Lawrence's portrayal of **Elizabeth** is based on his mother, who was better educated than her husband and had been a pupil-teacher[8] but was reduced to working as a home-worker in the

---

[7] *"American cloth"* – a new imported cloth from America, cheap, easy to clean and hardwearing. It was the ubiquitous covering for kitchen tables until well after the second world war in lower and middle class households where eating was done mainly in the kitchen.

[8] A pupil who stays on at school and is trained to teach younger children, before there were teacher training colleges and before education was

lace industry of Nottingham. It was she who gave Lawrence his love of books and the opportunity to move away from the mining life, when he was awarded a scholarship to Nottingham High School.

Elizabeth is of a disillusioned woman, disappointed in her life and her marriage, which has made her *"bitter"*. Much of the time, this *"bitterness"* is kept under tight control, for the sake of her children and for pride – she will not admit to anyone, even her father, that her husband is a drunk and that she cannot rely on him for his support. This pride is evident in Lawrence's first description of her: *"imperious"* is from the same root as *"imperial"*, meaning that she sees herself as having power and control; her eyebrows are *"definite"* and her hair is *"parted exactly"* (lines 26 – 28). This is a woman who has standards that she is determined to maintain, even if though she is trapped by poverty and the low expectations of women whose purpose is to cook, clean and sleep with their husbands.

Elizabeth is set apart from the other women in the story by her language, her actions and her setting. She does not speak in the strong dialect of the other women – or even her father - but in a modified Standard English, indicating that she has received more education. She insists to herself that she will not go to the Prince of Wales pub to *"fetch him"* (line 220) as the other women would if their husbands did not come home because they were on a bender. She hesitates to even ask her neighbours for help, until fear overcomes her pride. The neighbour recognises that Elizabeth is not like them; she is spoken to in a *"tone tinged with respect"* (line 227) and *"with deference and sympathy"* (line 255). However, the women and their husbands rally to support Elizabeth in her time of trouble, searching out her husband and

universal.

ensuring that someone is with her when he is brought home, showing how close knit the mining communities were.

The difference between Elizabeth and the other miner's wives is also shown in the contrast between her neat, orderly household and the chaotic mess of the miner's wife's home, even though she acknowledges that the twelve children makes this mess *"No wonder!"* In this contrast between the miner's wife *"twelve"* and Elizabeth's two, (soon to be three), children, there is a suggestion that Elizabeth has also been careful not to allow the endless cycle of pregnancy and birth, year on year, to happen to her, although she has been married long enough for her eldest child to be at school.

Elizabeth is also associated with the dark. She puts the coals on the fire *"piece after piece"* until the room is almost in *"total darkness"* (line 140-141). She speaks of meeting and fighting, metaphorically, with her husband *"in the dark"* (503). In darkness, she can hide her inner thoughts and feelings. Darkness also hides the harsh reality of her relationship with her husband.

The death of her husband frees Elizabeth – not from hardship (she agonises over whether she can support her family on *"the little pension and what she could earn"* line 324), but from hiding from herself that their life together failed to fulfil either of their needs. She has been aware that her life was far from ideal – she herself says *"what a fool I've been, what a fool!"* (line 174) - but the awfulness of his death enables her to acknowledge openly to herself the gulf between them, and that they were strangers to each other. Death *"restored the truth"* (line 512). She is able, at last, to feel *"grief and pity"* for him, that he should have died without living a life in which his own individual wants and needs could be expressed openly, be acknowledged and fulfilled. Her pity is as much for him as it is for herself.

The children, John and Annie, are clearly, if quickly, characterised as miniature versions of their parents. John is sullen and taciturn, like his father, and clearly resentful of his father's absence and uncomfortable with his mother or the atmosphere of hostility that he can sense. His voice is *"sulky"* (line 32), he *"tears"* at the chrysanthemums. His mother sees herself in his *"silence and pertinacity"* and his father in his *"indifference to all but himself"* (line 93). The child is set apart from his parents, exhibiting the strangeness that at the end Elizabeth sees in her husband – a being totally other than herself. This idea of the child being alien is in the description of him hiding in the dark and under the sofa and creeping out *"like a frog"* (line 190).

The girl, Annie, is a life-affirming symbol of hope. Her mother hears her footsteps *"gratefully"* (line 103), although she hides her feelings by pretending to be cross with her for being late. The promise for the future lies in the *"curls ripening from gold to brown"* (line 105), an image of bounty and plenteousness. She also notices the chrysanthemums in her mother's waistband with *"rapture"*; they are an unexpected note of brightness in her mother's usually solemn appearance and she takes an innocent pleasure in the flowers, which have no unwelcome connotations as they have for the mother. Annie delights in gazing into the fire, which feeds her imagination, seeing in it *"caves"* (line 126). Her life is ahead of her, for her to make of it what she will, hopefully untainted by others' expectations of her and free of the disappointments of her mother's life.

Themes, Symbolism and Imagery

The main symbol lies in the title *"Odour of Chrysanthemums"*. An odour is a smell which will linger even after the flowers that produced them have gone, a symbol of Elizabeth and Walt's **dying relationship with each other**. We first encounter the chrysanthemums in the scrubby garden, their *"dishevelled"* flowers looking like *"cloths hung on bushes"* (line 23), which her son absent-mindedly *"tears"* at, perhaps as he worries about the relationship between his parents, and his father's absence.

Her daughter takes an innocent delight in the flowers in her mother's waistband and her urging of her mother not to *"take them out"* (line 162) suggests that she sees still the possibility of a happier future for her mother – or a memory of the young girl that her mother was. Elizabeth hates the flowers. To her they are **a symbol of her disappointment and mark the deterioration of her marriage**. Initially, perhaps, a token of love and affection (*"when I married him"* and *"when you were born"*), they have become symbols of the separation between them (*"first time they ever brought him home drunk...brown chrysanthemums in his buttonhole"* lines 167-169). They are in a vase in the parlour where they take Walt's body for laying out, their bitter smell *"deathly"*. Finally, they lie on the floor amongst the shards of smashed glass which Elizabeth clears away before they lay out her husband's body, as a symbol of their broken life together.

Links

"Odour of Chrysanthemums", *"Korea"* and *"A Family Supper"* are all **domestic dramas** which explore **familial relationships** and reveal **the tensions** below the surface.

"Odour of Chrysanthemums" explores **female sexuality**. The Mother in *"Chemistry"* and Elizabeth, are struggling with their sexuality; the Mother gives in to her need for a partner, Elizabeth wonders how she can have made love to someone she barely knew. Sandra, in *"The Darkness Out There"* is a young girl on the verge of womanhood whose ideas of men and sex is based on childhood fantasies but whose experience in the cottage shows her a future reality.

As in *"Invisible Mass of the Back Row"*, *dialect* is used to explore themes of **Identity**.

My Polish Teacher's Tie – Helen Dunmore

Context

Helen Dunmore is a poet, as well as a writer of short stories and novels. This story was included in her collection *"Ice Cream"* published in 2003.

The link between the UK and Poland goes back to the Second World War, when Britain, having pledged to defend Poland from invasion by Nazi Germany, entered the war when Poland was invaded in 1939. Many Polish aircraftmen flew their planes to England and fought alongside the RAF. They were the fourth largest group of Allied forces. After the war, more than 100,000 displaced Polish servicemen, and others who had made their way out of Poland, remained behind as Poland became annexed by Russia. The 1947 Polish Resettlement act allowed them to remain and apply for full citizenship. Immigration continued after the war, and accelerated with the fall of Communism in 1989, which enabled freer travel. Poland joined the EU in 2004, which brought further immigration. It is now estimated that around one million Poles live in Britain, the largest overseas group of UK residents.

The mother of the narrator of the story came to Britain *"after the war"* and married an Englishman. The story perhaps reflects attitudes to immigrants in the 1990s, before the accession of Poland to the EU, when there were fewer Poles in Britain, hence the casual racism of the teachers and Carla's feelings of alienation from her colleagues and society in general.

Dunmore portrays Stefan as "an innocent abroad"[9], drawing on a literary convention much used by American writers of the late 19th – early 20th centuries, such as Mark Twain and Henry James.

---

[9] From *"The Innocents Abroad"* by Mark Twain (1869) which is a travelogue documenting Twain's travels by boat around Europe and the Near East.

In these writings, a naive young man travels from the stereotypically simpler, less sophisticated, society of America (the "new world") to the more cultured and sophisticated, but ultimately corrupt, society of Europe (the "old world"). In so doing, he shows that his homespun values of truthfulness, honesty and plain-speaking can overcome the prejudices of privilege and wealth. Dunmore places Stefan as the innocent, in this case from Poland, travelling to England, which is hidebound by hierarchy, status and prejudice against "foreigners". He overcomes all, and rescues Carla in the process, with his child-like innocence, symbolised by his *"terribly hopeful tie"*.

Plot and Plot Structure

The story is told in *linear time*. Part of the narrative is *epistolary*, written as a series of extracts from letters between Carla, the narrator, and Stefan ("Steve"), her pen-friend.

Carla is the daughter of a Polish woman and English father. She learned Polish as a child until her father *"put a stop to it"*. She works as *"part-time catering staff"* (what used to be called a *"dinner lady"*) at a school. She has a child, Jade, but there is no mention of a partner. When she overhears the Headmaster asking for a *"penfriend"* for a teacher in Poland, prior to a proposed teacher-exchange programme, she plucks up courage to ask for the address and begins to write to him, keeping her role in the school secret. They exchange news and she reminisces about her childhood learning Polish songs. Steve sends her poetry, one based on her stories of her early life.

Some months later, it is announced that Stefan is to visit, staying with one of the teachers. Carla panics, assuming that the somewhat formal tone of Stefan's last letter reflects his feelings of disappointment that she did not offer to accommodate him on his visit. However, he looks forward to meeting her and her colleagues. She imagines the scene when her role is revealed.

She stops writing to him and thrusts the impending visit out of her mind.

She is, therefore, taken by surprise one day at break, overhearing the teachers talking about Stefan. She has not noticed that he is in the staffroom. She looks at him from across the room, noticing his *"terribly hopeful tie"*. She abandons her place behind the counter and goes over to meet him. They shake hands and then Stefan starts singing a song that she remembers from her childhood and she joins in. In so doing, she finally comes to terms with her identity. The story ends with her complimenting Stefan on his tie.

Narrative Perspective and Voice

The story is a *first-person narrative*, told by the main *protagonist*, Carla. To an extent, like the boy in *"Chemistry"*, Carla is an *unreliable narrator*. Dunmore creates Carla to explore themes of **identity and self.** Her feelings of inferiority, and crisis of confidence, are bound up with her **confusion over her identity**. She lives between the "old world" of her birthplace and the "new world" of her mother's. Carla's view of her world is distorted by her own feelings of inadequacy. She projects these feelings onto her interactions with others which potentially gives her a biased view of her colleagues, and leads to a misinterpretation of Stefan's motivations and feelings. Dunmore shows this through the creation of Carla's *narrative voice*, which is initially sarcastic and scathing of herself and others. Only when she reconnects to her linguistic and cultural heritage, when she finds again her "mother-tongue", it is suggested, does she speak in her authentic "voice".

Carla's feelings of inferiority are evident from the opening where she defines herself by her *"uniform"* and the amount she is paid: *"that's me. £3.89 per hour"*. She is disparaging about the teachers, as evident from her choice of words to describe her job:

"*I dish out tea and buns*", the "*dish out*" making it sound crude and thoughtless, whilst the reference to "*buns*" is almost certainly an echo from her, and Dunmore's, childhood when children visiting London Zoo were able to feed "*buns*" to the elephants, thus dehumanising the teachers (lines 1 – 3). Her contempt for her job (and herself?) is also evident in the word "*shovel*" to describe serving up the chips (line 2). She also makes a clear distinction between the teachers and the "*kids*", her statement "*I like the kids*" (line 3) being deliberately set by Dunmore as a short, simple sentence at the end of the paragraph, to make the distinction clear.

This characterisation of Carla as having a "chip on her shoulder", and thus distorting her view of those around her, continues in the second paragraph where she refers to visitors having to pay for their tea "*or it wouldn't be fair*", adopting a phrase she has heard the teachers use. She scathingly comments on the teachers' system by saying "*Very keen on fairness, we are, here*" (line 6), the "*we*" identifying herself with the teachers ironically, as she has clearly established that she feels no kinship with them at all. This sarcastic tone continues in paragraph 7, where she throws out the comment "*Teachers are used to getting out of the way......*" (line 22), and again when she refers to the Headmaster: "*He stitched a nice smile on his face...*" (line 25), the word "*stitched*" suggesting that the smile is false.

This bitter tone continues until she reconnects with her Polish mother's teaching through her letters to Stefan and her *idiolect* takes on a more lyrical, unselfconscious tone as her pent-up feelings pour out of her: "*I told him about Jade. I told him about the songs...*" (line 47).

Finally, she reverts to her "mother-tongue", uniting with Stefan in a Polish song, remembered from childhood, which brings a resolution as she discovers her authentic "voice", a voice that she thought she had forgotten.

Setting

Setting plays little part in the effectiveness of the story, other than by its absence. Dunmore shows that Carla is not interested in her physical surroundings; her focus is on her interaction with the people around her as these are the source of her discomfort and feelings of inferiority.

Characterisation

Carla is primarily characterised through her *narrative voice*, but we also learn about her from her interactions with the other teachers and the Headmaster, from occasional memories recounted, and from her letters.

Carla's first name is not revealed until line 75, when we hear it in a letter from Stefan; she is referred to as *"Oh, er – Mrs, er – Carter"* (line 26) by the Headmaster and *"Mum"* by her daughter. This lack of first name further strips Carla of identity.

We learn that she is the daughter of a Polish mother, who came to the UK after the second world war, and a British husband, who disapproved of his daughter being taught Polish. This was a not uncommon attitude in the second half of the 20th century, before the benefits of being bilingual in a modern world were realised or valued. This disapproval began the process of alienating Carla from her cultural heritage and identity, leaving her feeling neither Polish nor British, and to her lacking a sense of self and developing feelings of inferiority.

The process of rediscovering her "self" begins with the letters to and from Stefan, as she reconnects thorough them to her heritage and her language. However, her new "self" is shown as being still fragile, as she attributes the apparent "stiffness" of Stefan's letter announcing his visit, to her not offering him a place to stay. She also describes herself as *"the person...who didn't really exist"*, reflecting her feeling that in writing to Steve in her emerging, private voice, she is still at odds with the public *persona* that exists at the school and that he will be unable to reconcile them when they meet (line 81). She imagines a nightmare scenario where she is humiliated in front of the teachers in Stefan's presence, demonstrating that her acquired feelings of inadequacy are deeply ingrained and affect her ability to connect with others, without attributing unkind motives to them.

The spur to her finally claiming an identity for herself is the casually racist comments of the teachers, who are commenting on Stefan. Ironically, it is being Polish that makes him invisible to them as an individual, whereas it is her feeling that she lacks a national identity that has led to her being invisible to them as an individual.

The Headmasters and Teachers are characterised almost entirely through Carla, in her unkind characterisations of them, in her reporting of conversations and her interactions with them. They are portrayed by Carla as hierarchical, seeing people in her position as of a lower status than themselves, and treating her with indifference. She portrays the Headmaster as something of a "bumbling" fool, with his hesitancy over her name (line 26), his "*wagging*" (lines 18 and 124) and "*flapping*" (line 146) of his papers.

In commenting on Stefan's accent and habits, the teachers exhibit the kind of casual racism, and simple bad manners, born of ignorance and complacency, perhaps more common at the time than now. An opposing view is proffered by Susie, who challenges their bigotry, pointing out that although he knows English poets, they know no Polish ones. Although undeveloped, this exchange suggests the awareness of a "new order".

Carla is particularly unkind about Valerie Kenward, who invites Stefan to stay with her. Her comments are not untinged with jealousy over Valerie's appropriation of "her" penfriend. She says she *"never liked"* her, accusing her of being always *"on a diet"* but *"taking the biggest bun."* Later, she is described as having *"poked"* the buns, but taking one anyway. Carla also passes judgement on Valerie's children, brought up to be *"pleased with themselves"*. Valerie is the embodiment of the "old world" – complacent, self-satisfied and prejudicial, unable to adapt to new experiences and a new world order.

We learn of **Stefan** through his letters and his appearance in the staff room at the end, in his *"terribly hopeful tie"* (line 127). Even though he changes his name in his letters to *"Steve"*, in keeping with his temporary "English" identity, the tie is a bold assertion of his sense of self and his individuality.

Stefan's portrayal as *"the innocent abroad"* is evident in the contrast between his knowledge of English, his letters about poetry and his support for Carla, which show education, confidence and generosity, and his feelings of bewilderment in the staff room. Here, he is in a world he does not understand and which does not understand him. He does not fit, like his *"too big"* suit (line 125). His difference from the society in which he finds himself is shown in Carla's description of the *"fantastic shine"* on his shoes, the word *"fantastic"* suggesting unreal, other-worldly, and his *"too open"* child-like face in an *"adult body"* (lines 127-128) characterising him as an alien being.

His innocence and openness are made evident when he sees Carla: *"He couldn't hide anything"*, unlike her, who has become adept at *"hiding"* her true self.

Carla is able to overcome her feelings of inadequacy and inferiority in defence of Stefan. In reaching out to him, where he stands adrift in the staffroom, *"hoping for rescue"*, she rescues herself.

Themes, Symbolism and Imagery

The story is concerned with ideas of **Identity** and how **Identity is formed by nationality, culture and language.** It also explores how **Identity is linked to Self,** but is separate from it. Carla, in struggling to find a national or cultural identity, also loses her sense of "self" – the person she is that transcends these labels. This is evident from the final lines of the story.

The *"first poem"* Stefan sends Carla is about a canary in a coal mine (line 47). Canaries were cage birds sent down the mines to test whether the air was safe. They were also kept as pets as they have a beautiful song. The canary can be seen as a symbol for Carla's **loss of identity** which is bound up in her loss of her "mother-tongue" or voice. She can hear it, just as she can hear the Polish in her head, and is searching for it, but cannot find it.

This idea is developed in the second poem Stefan sends, about Carla being *"half-Polish and half English."* (line 57). Again, he refers to the *"loss"* of the *"words"* her Mother gave her.

Carla's sense of self re-emerges when she stands up to Valerie Kenward, leaving her *"with her mouth ...still open"* (line 131). In singing the Polish song together at the end, Carla rediscovers her "voice" and her identity, the repeated *"I knew it, I knew it"* showing her wonder and delight. She makes an open declaration of Identity to the Headmaster when he admits to not realising she was Polish: *"Nor did I, I said."* (line 147).

The image of the tie is central to this theme of **Identity** and **Self.** Carla sees it as *"terribly hopeful"*, reflecting Stefan's innocence in not believing, or not caring, that this tie will mark him out as "other" and open to ridicule, as Valerie's comments confirm: *"And his ties!" went on Valerie. "You've never seen anything like them."* (line 121).

In describing the tie as a *"flag"*, but not one which represents a particular nationality (its lack of definition is evident in the word *"squiggles"*), Dunmore broadens the image to comment on **Self**. Stefan's tie is *"much too wide and much too bright"* to simply declare him as "Polish". It is a flag from *"another country, a better country than the ones either of [them] lived in"* (line 149), where there is difference and conflict. In saying *"I like your tie,"* Carla transcends their national and cultural identities to affirm their shared humanity.

Links

Ideas of **Identity** are central to *"Invisible Mass of the Back Row"*, where Hortense finds a new cultural identity through reading about Black History. Cultural identity is also at the centre of *"A Family Supper"* where the boy and girl both see themselves as being restricted by traditional Japanese culture and attribute motives to their father based on their understanding of that culture, rather than the man himself.

Ideas of **Self** are central to *"Odour of Chrysanthemums"*, in Elizabeth's realisation of the impossibility of ever truly knowing another person. This idea is also developed in *"Korea"*, where the boy is faced with the realisation that he has never known or understood his Father. A similar theme runs through *"A Family Supper"*, when the Father expresses surprise at his son's suggestion that he condoned the suicide and murder of his old business partner, and in *"The Darkness Out There"*, where the true nature of both the boy, Kerry, and the old woman, Mrs Rutter, are utterly unknown, and unknowable, to the protagonist, Sandra.

Korea – John McGahern

Context

John McGahern was an Irish writer who drew on his experiences growing up in rural Ireland. McGahern's mother, a primary school teacher, died of cancer when he was ten and he and his six siblings, all girls, moved to live in barracks with his father, who was a sergeant in the Garda[10] and who had fought in the Irish War of Independence for the Republicans. Reportedly, his father was a brutal man with a violent temper who physically abused the children. McGahern did well at school, and as a result became a school teacher himself. These experiences permeate his writing.

McGahern's second novel, *"The Dark"* (1965) was banned in Ireland for obscenity and led to McGahern being dismissed from his job as a teacher, on the direct orders of the then Archbishop of Dublin. McGahern moved to England, where he remained for nearly a decade until his return to Leitrim, near where he grew up. His novel *"Amongst Women"* (1990) was short-listed for the Mann-Booker prize. *"Korea"* was published in the volume of short stories *"Nightlines"* (1970) and made into a film in 1995, starring Andrew Scott.[11]

There are two wars referenced in the short story. The first, where the Father sees the execution, is the Irish War of Independence (1919-1921) in which the Irish Republican Army (IRA) fought a guerrilla war against the British, a prelude to the formation of the Irish Free State. Under the Anglo-Irish Treaty of 1921, 26 Irish counties became independent of British rule, the remaining six forming what is now Northern Ireland, part of the UK. The

---

[10] The *Garda* are the police force of Ireland.
[11] Andrew Scott is now famous for playing Moriarty in BBC TV's production of *"Sherlock"* (2010-2017) with Benedict Cumberbatch and as the "new broom" C in the James Bond film *"Spectre"* (2015)

second, the Korean War (1950-1953) followed the invasion of South Korea by North Korea. Korea had become split after the Second World War; the Soviet Union had liberated the North from Japan at the end of the war, and US forces had occupied the South. Neither side recognised the boundary between the two as permanent. Following the invasion, the UN authorised UN troops to support the South, of which the US provided nearly 90% of the military personnel. The armistice of July, 1953, formed a demilitarised zone between the two. A peace treaty has never been signed.

Millions of Irish have emigrated to America since the mid-19th century, mostly as economic migrants. Around 10 percent of the population claims Irish ancestry. Emigrants from Ireland domiciled in the US at the time of the Korean war either volunteered for duty or were drafted. An entry in the New York Times dated February 3rd, 1952, records a service in St Patrick's Cathedral for nine young Irish -born emigrants who were drafted into the army and died during the war. Their bodies were repatriated to their places of birth in Ireland.[12]

Plot and Plot Structure

The story opens with the boy retelling his father's account of the execution of a young man and a boy that he witnessed during the Irish War of Independence. The father then tells directly the effect the sight had on him years later, when he was reminded of the incident on honeymoon. The father then makes a seemingly casual enquiry as to what his son wants to do when he leaves school when he gets his exam results that summer. He suggests that his son might consider going to America, the *"land of opportunity"*. The boy is puzzled but says he will *"think about it"*.

---

[12] http://www.illyria.com/irishkor.html

The exchange takes place while the two are night-fishing for eels, which they send weekly to Billingsgate Market in London to supplement their income from their farm. They fish for the eels in a local river, baiting the lines of hooks with worms. They are the last to family to fish on this river – it is unlikely that the man's licence will be renewed, as it interferes with tourism, a sign of the changes coming to Ireland. The boy feels guilty about leaving, as he realises that his father will face economic hardship.

During that day, the father works in the potato fields while the boy replaces the hooks on the line and digs for worms. Whilst storing the worms in the outside lavatory, the boy overhears his father talking to a local cattle-dealer about a local boy, Luke Moran, who died in Korea, fighting in the US army. He hears that each soldier is insured for $10,000, which goes to the family on his death, and that the families of serving soldiers receive a monthly allowance from the US Government. The boy believes that his father's suggestion that he go to America is in the hope that he will reap the rewards for his service, or death, if his son is drafted.

That night, while eel fishing, the boy asks his father if he thinks much about the war he took part in, to which the father replies that he wished he'd focused on his own troubles, leaving the country to fend for itself, as he would be *"better off"* had he done so.

Narrative Perspective and Narrative Voice

The tale is told as a *first-person narrative* by the son. There is considerable switching between recount of events, *interior monologue* (where the son comments on his interpretation of his father's words and the effect they have on him), and dialogue. The opening recount of the execution is retold by the son, perhaps to make it more shocking, but also in contrast to the father's recollection of the incident *"years after"*, where the memory is vividly recalled by the sight of the popping *"furze[13]-pods"*, which *"destroyed the day"*. There is considerable dialogue, in which we hear the father's voice, but his words are often immediately qualified by the son, as when he remarks *"there was something calculating in the face"*. This makes the truth of the son's interpretation of events open to question – our view of the father is always filtered through the son's perceptions.

Setting

McGahern's writing records the hard life of Irish farmers after the war. They had little education, large families and survived on subsistence-level farming. This setting is the driving force of the plot. It records a fast-disappearing world; the children of these men, like the boy and McGahern himself, were better educated and planned to move away from home and off the land. The traditional way of life is carefully, and minutely, detailed by McGahern in sensuous, descriptive writing. His description of working man in a landscape is similar to DH Lawrence's in *"Odour of Chrysanthemums"*. He conjures up the sounds of the river and their eel-fishing: the *"slow ripple of oars"*, *"the lowing of cattle"*, *"the wings of duck shirred."* He describes the landscape in which they work as a place of beauty: the baited line *"throbbed"* with fish (line 36), the line is *"beaded with running drops of water"* (line 46). This is in contrast to the *"ugly whirls"* of the bats (line 107) and the *"smell of shit and piss and...worms crawling"* (line 94) which hint at the darkness beneath the deceptively calm surface.

---

[13] *Furze,* also known as *gorse,* is a bright yellow flower, which smells of coconut, that grows on prickly bushes on heathland. The seeds are contained in long pods, like pea-pods, which explode when ripe to disperse the seeds.

Characterisation

We learn little about **the Son**, other than that he is better educated than his father and looking to move away from the farm when he receives his exam results; it is his *"last summer with him on the river."* (line 34). He feels guilty at leaving life on the farm (line 78). He seems to be at ease with his father, but not close. In the final paragraph, he says: *"I'd never felt so close to him before"*, although they have shared happy experiences together, as in a sporting Final.

We learn about **the Father** through the son's observations and perceptions, through their dialogue and the Father's dialogue with the cattle-dealer, and through his recounting of the memories of the execution. McGahern makes the father's reactions to events, and his words, equivocal – open to interpretation, thus suggesting darker currents of feeling running below the surface of a seemingly innocent conversation.

The account of the execution is given, by the boy, with detachment, but the man's recollection of the aftermath in his memory is vivid, and uses an image which contrasts the ugliness of the death of the boy with a natural event which is surprisingly imaginative. His comment *"It destroyed the day"* (line 25), however, reveals a harsher, more self-pitying side to the man.

He seems to resent his son's education and the opportunities it brings him, *"aggressively"* suggesting that his son has been at school *"too long"* (line 31). The boy sees his enquiries into his plans as *"calculating"* and distrusts the sincerity of his enquiry about the possibility of the boy going to America: *"the words fumbled"* and he is *"wary of the big words… not in his voice"* (line 68). The son seems to hear a sales pitch being made. The father is also portrayed as a disappointed man who has worked hard all his life and has little to show for it. He clearly does not want his son to follow him and make the same mistakes.

On the other hand, there is admiration in the son's description of his father "*baiting each hook so beautifully*" (line 106) and dipping the oars in the water "*without a splash*" (line 111). He can appreciate mastery of a craft, even though he believes his father to be capable of a terrible betrayal.

The climax of the story comes with the overheard conversation between the Father and the cattle-dealer, at which they appear to be discussing the financial benefit to be gained by sending the boy off to America, if he were then to be drafted to fight in the Korean War. His father sounded "*excited*". The boy's appalled reaction, as he puts two and two together, is unsurprising, given that he can recall "Luke Moran" coming back home in a coffin. He sees this moment as the loss of innocence: "*I knew my youth had ended*" (line 104).

If the boy's interpretation of events is to be believed, there is an irony in the words of the Father when his son tells him he has decided not to go to America: "*It'll be your own funeral*" (line 116).

The final words of the father seem to be at odds with the boy's interpretation of his father's intentions for him. He admits to being upset by recounting the execution, the image of the dead boy's buttons staying with him. He also seems to reject going into battle for other people; he asserts that he should have "*fought [his] own wars*" and let Ireland "*fend for itself*". However, this could further emphasise the disconnect in the father's mind between what he is proposing for his own son (to fight in a foreign war) and the fate of the boy shot in the Irish war.

The final paragraph suggests that only now does the boy finally see his father for what he is. He feels he has "*never been so close*" to his father, as if the scales have fallen from his eyes and he sees his father for what he truly is – a man capable of "*murder*" - the word with which the story shockingly ends.

Themes, Symbolism and Imagery

This is another **domestic drama** which explores **familial relationships** and reveals **the tensions below the surface**. It is a story about **things hidden, deception** and **distortion** of the truth. It is also a **coming-of-age** story, or story of **innocence and experience**.

The imagery is drawn from fishing, the activity that the boy and his father share. The father can be seen as the *"twisted hook"*, the hook that he baits with worms *"so beautifully"*, with his talk of the promise of America. The father has become *"twisted"* by his disappointment with the harshness of his life and his financial insecurity. The eels in the wire cages that *"slide over each other in their own oil"* or the *"other fish"* in the boat, are sold off, like the son believes the father proposes to "sell off" his son, as the lost boys, Luke, Michael and Sam, have been "sold" to bring in money for their families. The bait, the *"crawling worms"*, that the boy sees just before he goes out to set the nightline, is his Father's apparent concern for his future and his suggestion that a better life is to be found in America. But these worms crawl *"in darkness"* – the darkness at the heart of the father's twisted soul.

They boy **"comes of age"** with the realisation of his father's deception: *"I knew my youth had ended"* (line 104). Until that point, he believed that he was part of the knowable, adult world, working alongside his father in his business and helping to keep it "afloat". When he overhears the conversation between his father and the cattle-dealer, he realises that, until that moment, he has been a naieve innocent.

Links

"A Family Supper" similarly deals with **things hidden below the surface** which are potentially fatal to family relationships, like the fugu fish lurks in its broth. The son, like Elizabeth in *"Odours of Chrysanthemums"*, or Sandra in *"The Darkness Out There"*, is

faced with the realisation that *"things are not as they seem"*. *"The Darkness Out There"* has a dark secret at its heart and explores the theme of hidden motivations beneath the *"creamy smiling pool"* of Mrs Rutter's face.

With the exception of *"Odour of Chrysanthemums"* and *"My Polish Teacher's Tie"*, all the stories in the collection could be regarded as **"coming-of-age"** stories in which a young person undergoes a traumatic or life-changing event and, as a result, enters into the adult world. This is also characterised as a **loss of innocence** and the **beginning of experience**.

A Family Supper – Kazuo Ishiguro

Context

Kazuo Ishiguro is a British writer whose family moved to Britain from Nagasaki, Japan, when he was five. They expected to return, and Ishiguro says he *"is not entirely like English people because...[he] was brought up by Japanese parents in a Japanese speaking home."*[14] He describes his Japanese as *"terrible"* and he writes in English. He acknowledges that he writes in the Western literary tradition, rather than the Japanese, although he is a fan of Japanese film. Ishiguro has written relatively few novels, perhaps the most famous being *"The Remains of the Day"* (1989), which won the Booker Prize, and *"Never Let Me Go"* (2005), a novel about clones. Both were made into films. *"A Family Supper"* was first published in 1982[15], when Ishiguro was 28 and before he returned to Japan, for the first time, for a visit. He has said that his first two novels were set in *"an imaginary Japan"*.

The story makes a number of references to Japanese culture. Ishiguro has commented on his intentions when writing this story: *"I suppose...I was consciously playing on the expectations of a Western reader. You can trip the reader up by giving out a few omens. Once I set the expectation about the fugu fish up, I found I could use that tension and that sense of darkness for my own purposes."*[16] These "expectations" include notions of Japanese honour which are associated with suicide – *hara-kiri* and *kamikaze*, the first a Samurai ritual killing by disembowelment, the second when pilots flew their aircraft into battleships during the second world war. By extension, Ishiguro suggests the fugu fish as a method of suicide.

---

[14] Graham Swift on Ishiguro *Bomb* magazine 1989
[15] In the journal, *Firebird 2*, although other sources say 1980 in *Quarto*
[16] Brian W. Shaffer and Cynthia F. Fong, Conversations with Kazuo Ishiguro (Jackson: University Press of Mississippi, 2008):

Plot and Plot Structure

The story opens with an explanation of the dangers of eating *fugu* fish, a Japanese delicacy. It is explained that the fish has to be prepared carefully, as the sexual glands of the fish contain a deadly poison. Death is not immediate, but occurs after some hours of agony. After the war, there was a short-lived craze of playing a kind of "Russian roulette" with eating the fish, before its sale and preparation were regulated.

The narrator is the son of a Japanese family who returns to Tokyo, Japan, from California, to visit his father and sister, two years after the death of his mother. Relationships with his family had become *"somewhat strained"*, delaying his visit. He learns that his mother died from eating fugu fish.

The son learns that his father's former business partner committed suicide when their business failed. As a result, his father has retired and clearly hopes that his son will return to live at home.

While their father prepares supper, the son and daughter, Kikuko, walk in the garden. The daughter is at university in Osaka. It is evident that she thinks and behaves like a modern young woman, as she smokes, has a boyfriend and is thinking of joining him in America. All this she has kept hidden from her father. She reveals that the business partner, before committing the Samurai ritual of *hara-kiri,* gassed his wife and children. There is a well in the garden and Kikuko recalls the night the son claims to have seen the ghost of an old woman in a white kimono nearby. Their mother said it was an elderly neighbour taking a shortcut through their garden, but neither of them seem to believe it.

Returning to the house, where supper is nearly ready, the father asks Kikuko to finish the vegetables while he and his son take a tour of the house. The father tells the son that he believes his mother took her life, disappointed that her son had left home. He shows the son the plastic models of battleships he makes, now that he has spare time, and reveals that he would have preferred to have fought in the air-force rather than the navy, as that would have given him a chance of using *"the final weapon"* – kamikaze.

The two join Kikuko for supper. The room is dark. In the shadows, the son catches sight of a photograph of an old woman in a white kimono and is told it is his mother, just before she died.

There is little discussion during supper. The main course is a pot of soup with fish, which they serve to one another. At the end, the son asks how his father felt about his partner's actions in killing his family and is surprised that his father thinks he was wrong. The father again asks his son if he will be staying in Japan, but when he gets no definite answer, expresses his hope that Kikuko will come home when she finishes her studies.

The story is notable for its delayed reveal of the details of events that happened in the past. This creates a feeling that not everything is as it appears to be at first, and creates the rising tension towards the climax of the family supper of the title. The mother's death is presented as an accident, and only later as a possible suicide, although the "how?" is left unexplained. The appearance of the ghost by the well is left as a childish tale, until the son sees the photograph later and it takes on a new significance. Details of the death of the business partner are left out by the father, and only given later by the daughter. The father's comments on his business partner's *"principles"* and comment that he *"admired"* him suggest that he believes the suicide was a noble act. The son is surprised, later, by his father's rejection of the code of honour. All these delays create the tension about the fish served at supper – is this to be a delayed reveal about the fugu fish with which the story opened? Have they all been poisoned?

Narrative Perspective and Narrative Voice

Readers instinctively align themselves with the narrator; we see events unfolding through the narrator's eyes and tend to "believe" what he tells us. As critical readers, we have to determine the extent to which the narrator is reliable, the author's intentions and where the truth lies. In his comments on his intention in writing the story, Ishiguro admits to *"playing"* with the reader. The narrative voice can be seen as part of his intent to deceive and lead astray – or *"trip [us] up"*.

The story is told in the first-person by the son. After the initial exposition about the *fugu* fish, much of the narrative is in the form of dialogue. The defining characteristic of the narrator is his detachment, created by the almost total absence of reflection on the events that occur. We never hear what he thinks or feels about his father, his sister, the death of his mother or the events that have occurred in his absence. This characterises the narrator as cut off from his past by time and distance. The effect is to give the sense that what the son reports may not be the whole story, enabling Ishiguro to "play" with the reader. Much of the tension in the story is created by *inference*[17], through setting and imagery, rather than by what we learn from the narrator.

Setting

Setting is used to create atmosphere and tension and to underpin the ritualistic aspects of Japanese culture. There is little detailed description. Ishiguro places the initial conversation between the father and son sitting on the *"tatami floor of his tearoom"* (line 18), a formal setting which emphasises the distance between the two. Much of the story takes place in semi-darkness to suggest things hidden and give a sense of foreboding. The garden outside the tea-room had *"fallen into shadow"* (line 41); the daylight has

---

[17] *Inference* means things suggested but not explicitly said or explained

almost gone as he walks in the garden with his sister and the light had grown *"very dim"* (line 123). They eat supper in a room lit by a lantern that casts the room into shadow. These shadows are deceptive and confusing. The son sees his father's face as *"stony and forbidding in the half-light"* (line 194) but he is revealed as a man grieving his wife and missing the company of his children; the darkness causes the son not to recognise the woman in the photograph as his mother; the son stares into the *"darkness"* (lines 255 and 262) of an unknown future. As he says, Ishiguro uses this *"darkness"* to create expectations of the outcome of the story.

Characterisation

Ishiguro sets up expectations of **the father** through the son's observations, which we later find may be overly judgemental. He describes his father's features as *"stony"* and *"furious"* (line 21), which suggests a hard, unfeeling nature. The comparison to "Chou En-Lai" is unflattering, as Chou was Chinese and Premier to Chairman Mao, the instigator of the Cultural Revolution, in which millions were executed or died. His pride is explained by his *"pure samurai blood"*. The samurai were the military office class of Japan up until the end of the 19th century, suggesting the father lives in the past and adheres to old codes of honour. The son recalls being *"struck"* for talking too much, explaining the silences between them.

However, as the story unfolds, we are shown another side to the man, through dialogue, which is less harsh. He misses his business partner and his wife. In revealing his suspicions about his wife's death, he shows his vulnerability, explaining his feelings of loss at the departure of his son to a world he does not understand. There is something touching about the formerly successful businessman making plastic models of battleships – and regretting his role in the war. He has, albeit reluctantly, learned to cook well. His repetition of *"she's a good girl"*, referring to Kikuko, reveals his fear that she too will leave, and leave him alone in his empty, too big, house.

Finally, the son is wrong in assuming that his father would endorse his business partner's actions in killing his wife and children before committing suicide. The father describes the action as being the result of *"weakened…judgement"* (line 249). Through the focus on an older world order of honour and codes, Ishiguro set up our expectations that the two older men would share the same view. Instead, the father wrong-foots the son, and the reader, by expressing surprise at the suggestion that he would think it anything other than *"a mistake"* (line 250). His declaration that *"There are other things beside work"* (line 253) shows that the father sees his first duty as being towards family, in spite of his apparent coldness towards them. This makes his wish that either, or both, his children would stay with him poignant, rather than selfish or domineering.

Kikuko is lightly characterised as a young girl torn between the traditional expectations of women in Japanese culture and the modern freedoms which women increasingly enjoy. She has "escaped" her father's old-fashioned notions by going to University, away from home, but feels the tug of tradition when she returns. She hides her smoking from her father, smoking in the garden and hiding the cigarette butt with pine needles; she has not told him about the boyfriend with whom she may go "hitchhiking" in America. She resents the assumption that her place is in the kitchen as when her father asks her, rather than her brother, to help with dinner and make the tea afterwards. The brother notices that she *"did not move"* (line 143) and she *"left the room without comment"* (line 240). The reader is left assuming that she will, indeed, follow her brother in leaving Japan.

Themes, Symbolism and Imagery

This is another **domestic drama** which explores **familial relationships** and reveals **the tensions** below the surface. It is a story about **things hidden, deception** and **distortion** of the truth. The story contrasts **the traditional with the modernist view** of the role of children, and of women, which, although set in Japan, is common across society. It explores the **tensions between cultural identity and self.**

It is also a "**coming-of-age**" story. The son, although an adult, still has much to learn about the motivations of adults and the nature of love, duty and honour. These are revealed to him by his father, about whom he discovers he knows very little.

A "family supper" is an event that symbolises closeness and shared family values as the generations come together to exchange their experiences, views and feelings[18]. This family supper is set in apparent opposition to this traditional view, as it is full of disappointment and unresolved tensions, and, instead of having a nourishing, healthy meal at its centre, the fish that lies hidden within the soup is potentially lethal.

The central image is the fugu fish, which, as Ishiguro says, "*sets up*" the expectations for the whole story. It is representative of Japanese tradition, and the family unit, which is at once wholesome, in binding Japanese society together, but it is also potentially poisonous, in stifling individual aspiration and self-determination. This tradition has been broken by the son leaving home for an American girl and it may be broken again by the daughter. One fish has already killed the mother, it is suggested. We are led to believe that the father may be about to kill the rest.

---

[18] For an understanding of the traditional "family supper", watch an episode of "*Blue Bloods*", a CBS television serial about an Irish-American police family. It is equally unrealistic, but provides an interesting contrast!

We are told that the fugu fish is potentially lethal - it all depends on the care with which it is prepared for eating. The poison of the fugu fish lies in the sex glands - a further development of the image to represent the son and daughter. There is an element of chance in whether you will be poisoned. The son is "*poisonous*" - he has been wrongly prepared by the parents who blame themselves for not *"bringing [him] up correctly"* (line 96), which led to him leaving home, breaking tradition and possibly leading to the "poisoning" of the mother through her suicide. Kikuko, on the other hand, has been properly prepared; she recalls her mother saying that her parents *"had been much more careful"* with her (line 97), which is why she is *"so good"*. She stills wrestles with the decision to leave or stay.

A further image lies in the ghost who is seen by the well. A well is a deep, dark place where the bottom is hidden from sight. If you drop a stone in the well, you have to wait for the splash, suggestive of time passing, but also inevitability. The ghost is an old woman in a kimono – the traditional Japanese dress which is rapidly giving way to clothes influenced by the West. In identifying the ghost with the mother, through the photograph, Ishiguro suggests that even when they were children, changes in Japanese society were inevitable – the death of traditional values, embodied by the mother, are foreshadowed by the appearance of the ghost and made manifest in the photograph seen years later, after the mother has died.

Links

Both *"Korea"* and *"A Family Supper"* explore the **relationship between fathers and sons**. *"Korea"* also uses images of fish under water to suggest **things hidden** below the surface of family relationships which lead to betrayal and disappointment.

The tension between an **identity** based on culture and a sense of **self** is explored in *"An Odour of Chrysanthemums"*, as Elizabeth wrestles with being a miner's wife, and in *"My Polish Teacher's Tie"* where Carla loses her sense of self by losing her cultural identity. *"Invisible Mass of the Back Row"* also explores how identity and culture are intertwined.

With the exception of *"Odour of Chrysanthemums"* and *"My Polish Teacher's Tie"*, all the stories in the anthology can be considered as *"***coming-of-age***"* stories or contrasting innocence with experience.

There are similarities between the narrative voice in *"Korea"* and *"A Family Supper"*, as both rely heavily on inference for effect.

Invisible Mass of the Back Row – Claudette Williams

Context

Claudette William's father left Jamaica for England in 1957, followed by her mother in 1960, making them amongst the first post-war immigrants from the Caribbean who were encouraged to emigrate to fill jobs in Britain. Claudette Williams was born in Heartsease, Jamaica, and lived with her Aunt until she joined her parents in England at the age of 10. The events of the story are based on her own experiences. It is set in the mid-1960s, with Hortense transitioning between primary school in Jamaica and secondary school in England.

The island of Jamaica, in the Caribbean, was initially inhabited by peoples from South America, the Arawak and Taino. It was colonised by the Spanish, following the arrival of Christopher Columbus in 1494, who enslaved those indigenous peoples who were not killed by disease, and who brought the first black Africans as slaves. It was ceded to the British in 1655 and became an important centre for the production of sugar cane, using thousands of black slaves. Slavery was abolished in 1834. Until 1962, when it gained independence, Jamaica was a British colony, ruled from the UK. It is now part of the Commonwealth, and a parliamentary democracy, with the Queen as its Head of State.

Until after the second world war, education in Jamaica was modelled on the British system. Although there was a comprehensive network of primary education, very few black Jamaicans progressed to secondary education and the majority of teachers were white, as there was no teacher training on the island until 1952. During the 1960s and 1970s there were a series of educational reforms to support the move towards political independence, including extending access to education beyond junior high school and the development of a curriculum that matched the needs of Jamaican children. The schooling Hortense received in England in the would have been familiar, as the curriculum and text books would have been very similar to those in use in Jamaica.

The story also touches on the issue of what has been called *"shadism"* – discrimination amongst peoples of African descent, in the Caribbean, and amongst African-Americans, based on the shade of their skin colour. This gained prominence recently with accusations that Beyoncé's skin had been artificially lightened, but the perceived superiority of Black people who have a lighter skin-tone goes back to the time of slavery. Slaves with a lighter skin colour tended to be employed as house-slaves, rather than in the fields. In turn, more light-skinned female slaves had children by their masters; these children were called *"mulatto"*. The children were more likely to be freed and accepted into the household of the master and left property and valuables on his death. There emerged an elite class of "light-skinned" people of African descent. It is this *shadism* to which Hortense refers when she calls Lorna a *"red pickney"* – a fair-skinned child[19].

The Black historical figures named by Hortense are:

Toussaint L'Ouverture (1743–1803) – leader of the Haitian Revolution against Napoleon, which instigated the fight for independence.
Sojourner Truth (1797-1883): abolitionist and activist, born into slavery in New York state, most famous for her abolitionist speech of 1851 *"Ain't I a woman?"*
Nanny or Queen Nanny of the Maroons (c.1686-c.1755) - National Hero of Jamaica - and *Captain Cudjoe* (c.1680-c.1744): leaders of

---

[19] A recent article on this issue can be found here:
https://www.theguardian.com/world/2011/oct/04/racism-skin-colour-shades-prejudice

the Jamaican Maroons, slaves who escaped and formed a self-governing colony in the hilly interior of the island.

Paul Bogle (1822-1865) – National Hero of Jamaica: Baptist deacon and activist who led a protest in 1865 against the British at Morant Bay. He was arrested, convicted under martial law and hung.

Plot and Plot Structure

The story opens *in media res*[20] with the protagonist, Hortense, who sits in the back row of her Year 6 class, transfixed by fear as she is asked to recite the story of Christopher Columbus by the school Inspector. Instead of giving the expected, and conventional answer, she blurts out her thoughts about Columbus's right to be in Jamaica, for which she receives a rap on the knuckles. She is saved from further punishment, literally, by the bell.

Hortense is seething with indignation and humiliation and decides to take it out on Lorna, a light-skinned (*"red"*) girl who sits in the front row. Her efforts to "get" Lorna are thwarted by the appearance of Teacher Edwards, who is not only dressed in a Dashiki suit, a traditional African garment (and a modern introduction to the Caribbean at that time) but is also *"beautifully dark"* (line 59). This, and his kind treatment of the children, make him a respected figure. But Hortense is still full of a feeling of injustice, which is directed towards the *"Inspector"* whom she characterises as "out-of-order" (*"renking, facety"* line 73), particularly as he is Black.

The children break for lunch and leave the school to go and buy food from the *"lunch women"*, local women who sell food to the children in the village. The feelings of humiliation gradually die down as the children jostle to buy food. But Hortense still

---

[20] *In the middle* – there is no exposition, as such.

wonders whether she will ever get to the "front row" of the class, and escape the humiliation of the Inspector's interrogation.

When she arrives at her Aunt's house, she finds a parcel waiting for her and news that she and her brothers are going to England to join their parents. On the November morning that they leave, Hortense finds "Cousy", an elderly relative, dead in bed, a symbol of her break with all she knows.

Hortense finds it hard to acclimatise to her new life, disliking the cold, the terraced housing (*"houses...stuck together"* line 200) and finding her parents little more than strangers to her. She finds familiarity in being in the metaphorical "back row" of her new secondary school, where she is in the second to bottom stream, and in her school-friends, many of whom are from the Caribbean, and use the same *patois* when speaking to one another. The girls have access to the library, where they begin to discover an alternative Black history which they can claim as their own.

When the dreaded question of Columbus comes up again in class, Hortense is ready with an answer. She recites what she has learned from reading the books, astonishing, and embarrassing, the teacher with her new-found "truth". Once again, the back row is saved by the bell and they troop out, leaving the teacher sitting transfixed to her desk, to celebrate their victory at finding their own, new "voice".

Narrative Perspective and Narrative Voice

The story is told as a *first-person narrative* by Hortense, who is based on Claudette Williams herself. We not only hear Hortense's account of the events, but are made aware throughout of her thoughts and feelings, which reflect and comment on her experiences. The voice is very different from the detachment of other first-person narratives, such as *"Korea"* and *"A Family Supper"* where there is little interior monologue and the reader has to deduce how the narrator feels from other clues, such as imagery and symbolism.

Hortense's *idiolect*[21] switches between Standard English and Jamaican *patois*. She slips between the two freely, as in lines 33-34, where she says that living with her aunt is like *"walking a tight-rope"* and then says of the incident in the school-room: *"Dis look and smell like big trouble to me"*. She also speaks Standard English to the teachers. Whilst the adult Hortense speaks in Standard English, the dialogue and Hortense's inner monologue is given to us in *patois*, which adds to the authenticity of her account[22]. This suggests that Hortense sees her *patois* as an assertion of her identity.

Setting

Setting is important in evoking the sights, sounds and smells of tropical Jamaica, in contrast to the cold of England, emphasising Hortense's feelings of alienation. Jamaica is primarily characterised through the sun and heat. Hortense's mental ordeal is intensified by the physical ordeal of the *"steam bath"* (line 24) of the school-room that causes the sweat to *"drip"* and *"flood"* her body. The smell of sweat is *"rank"*, strong and disgusting, adding to the humiliation. As they head for the airport, the sun *"releases its passions"* (line 147) and *"its enormous strength"* (line 168). The blue of the sea is said to *"retaliate"* (line 168), as in a battle, trying to outdo the brightness of the sun with its own *"bluest blue."*

The women at the foot of the cotton tree are vividly characterised through the senses, particularly smell. Miss Ivy wears her *"red tie-head"* (line 84), Aunt Dine *"smells of cinnamon"* and has *"toothless black gums"* (line 86). Miss Mavis has *"oiled, ivory*

---

[21] Her way of speaking
[22] A useful dictionary of *patois* can be found here:
http://niceup.com/patois.html

skin" and "*white, white eyes*" (line 91) whilst "*one-foot Herby*" trades "*sky-juice and snowball*" (line 95). "*Smells linger and whirl*" (line 100) as the food the children buy is listed to show the diversity and richness of the offerings, suggesting a life-force flowing through the community (lines 98 – 100).

The contrast with England begins as Hortense puts on her new clothes, which she feels "*gingerly*" (warily) and have "*new...smells*" (line 143). Williams lists the characteristics of cold England, the place of "*exile*" (line 186), each descriptive word and phrase separated on the page to convey Hortense's feelings of dislocation and alienation: "*paraffin heaters*", "*smell*", "*cold dark places*", "*afraid*", "*excited,*" "*cold*", "*smell*" "*wanting to be elsewhere,*" "*in fact Jamaica*" (lines 186-196).

Hortense creates a new setting of her own which perhaps reconciles these two worlds, by speaking *patois* to her friends and creating a corner of the common room "*dominated*" by new smells – "*hair pomander, face powder and Woolworth's fragrances*" (line 225). She also has the library which give her a new way of looking at the world.

Characterisation

Hortense is characterised by her *narrative voice*. She has a strong sense of *self*, but this is challenged by perceived injustices. She is abrasive, and angry. She uses her *patois* as a weapon, lashing out at her adversaries. She admits early on to being a "*rebel*" (line 13) and goes on the offensive. Her feelings of injustice go deep: she says she could "*kill*" her teacher (line 26); she declares that "*somebody has to pay*" for her humiliation and alights on Lorna Phillips, whom she threatens to give a "*bloody nose*" and "*beat up*" because she has a lighter skin and is rich (line 50); she rails at the "*warra warra*[23]" Inspector whom she feels has betrayed them.

---

[23] "*warra warra*" is a substitute for a range of swear words

This anger is fuelled by her uncle, who declares that everyone is against poor, black people like them.

Hortense is also a child who responds to warmth and kindness, whether it be the "*big and strong*" lunch women (line 83) or the "*warm bosom*" of her Cousy (line 163). She is seen surrounded by classmates who follow her lead, both in Jamaica and in England. The rebel has a voice that demands to be heard.

Themes, Symbolism and Imagery

The story shows how the "Invisible" can become "Visible" given the opportunity, how the "Mass" can resolve itself into the "Individual" and how the "Back Row" of history can be brought to the Front. The story is concerned with ideas of **Identity** and how **Identity is formed by nationality, culture and language.** It also explores how **Identity is linked to Self**, but is separate from it. The story is also about "**coming-of-age**".

Hortense is relegated to the back row because she is "black" (dark skinned as opposed to "*red*" or light-skinned) and poor. She describes herself as "*hidden, disposed of, dispatched*" (line 7). She contrasts herself with Lorna who is light-skinned and considers herself "*pretty*" (line 46). She looks for people like her in Teacher Edwards, who is "*beautifully dark*" and her sense of betrayal by the Inspector is intensified because "*After all him is suppose to be black*" (line 75). Her uncle accuses the Inspector of colluding with the teachers to humiliate "black" people like her, by never picking on the "*red pickney*", making it look as if only people like her "*no know nothing*" (line 78). This is a crisis of **self,** centred on her appearance and her poverty.

She is also challenged by her **cultural identity**, as she cannot reconcile the White, Eurocentric history she is taught in school with her (scant) knowledge of the history of indigenous and Black people in the Caribbean. She cannot find the words to articulate this – they *"tumble out"* of her, forming questions. But she is sufficiently indignant to try and give her frustration a voice.

Her move to England removes much of the anger centred on her skin colour – they are all now *"clearly black"* (line 222) compared with the white English. They are all poor, all recent immigrants from the Caribbean. She has moved *"one rung"* (line 222) up from the metaphorical "back row" of the Remedial class, but she sees herself as in *"familiar territory"*. Just as in the Caribbean girls like her resigned themselves to low-paid jobs, the girls ironically see themselves as *"graduating"* in the use of beauty products (line 225).

However, England brings access to a library. The library and the debates that follow supply Hortense with an alternative cultural history and give her a *"right to be"* (line 241). She is no longer relegated to the "back row" of history, nor invisible, not part of an anonymous mass of "black people", but can take centre stage, as the descendant of famous Black heroes *"Toussaint L'Ouverture, Sojourner Truth, Nanny, Cudjoe, Paul Bogle"* (line 241 – 242). This time, when the dreaded Columbus question is asked in class, the back row *"comes into its own"* (line 254). Hortense is now able to speak *"slowly and...well"* (line 259) telling the truth as they have discovered it for themselves from reading books.

Links

There are clear similarities with *"My Polish Teacher's Tie"* and *"A Family Supper"* in the exploration of **Identity and Self**. *"Odour of Chrysanthemums"* and *"My Polish Teacher's Tie"* also use language and *dialect* as key to forming Identity.

The theme of *"***coming-of-age***"* is shared with all the stories in the anthology, with the exception of *"Odour of Chrysanthemums"* and *"My Polish Teacher's Tie"*.

The Darkness Out There – Penelope Lively

Context

Penelope Lively is a Booker prize winner (with *"Moon Tiger"* in 1987) and Carnegie Medallist (for *"The Ghost of Thomas Kempe"* in 1973) who has produced a steady stream of acclaimed novels and short stories for adults and children. Her English parents were posted with an International bank in Cairo, Egypt, where she was born, and she was sent to England to boarding school when she was twelve. She studied modern history at Oxford and many of her novels are set in the past or explore the interplay between history and memory. The short story appeared in the collection *"A Pack of Cards: stories 1978 – 1986"* (1987).

Assuming that the date of the story is contemporary with the time of writing, it is set some thirty years after the end of the Second World War, which many people in their 60s and 70s would have experienced. Nearly 2000 Luftwaffe (the German air-force) planes were lost during the four months of the Battle of Britain in 1940; the number downed over Britain over the whole of the war was significantly higher, although figures are hard to confirm.

Plot and Plot Structure

Sandra, the main protagonist, goes to visit an old woman, Mrs Rutter, as part of her community service in the school's "Good Neighbour's Club". On the way, she has to pass close to Packer's End, a small wood, about which many stories have grown up over the years and which the local children avoid.

As she walks, she is surprised by Kerry Stevens, who is also in the club and has been assigned to visit with her. She is disappointed as she is not fond of Kerry and would have preferred to "have a laugh" with one of her girlfriends.

Mrs Rutter's cottage appears cosy, ornamented with china figures, although somewhat run down. While Mrs Rutter makes tea, Sandra cleans the kitchen and washes clothes and Kerry goes out to work in the yard. Mrs Rutter keeps up a constant monologue, commenting on Sandra's clothes and recounting the details of her marriage and the death of her husband in the war.

While they drink tea, Kerry asks about the story of the downed German plane that landed in the wood. Mrs Rutter tells them that she and her sister were in the cottage on the night it happened, that they had gone out to investigate and found one dead and one badly wounded German airman trapped in the wreckage. The boy was mumbling *"mutter, mutter"*[24] which she did not understand. As it was raining hard, they returned to the cottage. Mrs Rutter went out to the plane the next day to find the young airman still alive. She left him there, in revenge for her husband's death. She visited him again that evening and he was still alive; the next morning he was dead. Only then did she go and report the crash to the authorities.

Kerry and Sandra, horrified, hastily leave the cottage; Mrs Rutter is oblivious to their reaction and carries on nattering. Outside, Kerry expresses his horror at what he has heard. A suddenly older and wiser Sandra reflects on how Kerry has grown in stature and how you can never really know what darkness lies in the hearts of people.

The story is structured like a fairy-tale and uses many of its tropes. Fairy-tales, such as *"Goldilocks"* or *"Hansel and Gretel"*, are set in woods which have a cottage in the middle of them. In both these tales, the woods are dark and menacing and the cottage is inviting and contains food, which the children eat. However, in one there is a hidden danger in the bears, in the other, a wicked witch who traps the children. Fairy-tales often have a young girl as the main

---

[24] *"Mutter"* is German for *"Mother"*

protagonist, as in "*Goldilocks*" and "*Snow White*" (which also has a cottage in a wood), and the tales are essentially "*coming-of-age*" fables in which the girls move from a state of innocence to one of experience.

The fairy-tale associations are strengthened in the exposition by the tales that come out of Packer's Wood. First, the children imagine "*witches and wolves*" and trees that resemble "*faces and clawed hands*" like in Disney's film "*Snow White*" (line 43). Then they hear of the crashed plane, a mixture of fact and fiction, and then, as the girl grows older, scare stories about murderers and rapists derived from newspaper stories. The "*gypsies*" mentioned are a reference to a commonly-held belief at the time, that "gypsies" stole babies and young children. There was a popular song from earlier in the century to which Lively is probably referring, which was sung as a warning: "*My mother said/I never should/Play with the Gypsies/In the wood.*"

Narrative Perspective and Narrative Voice

The story is written in *third-person limited* – we only know how Sandra is thinking and feeling. Whilst the narrative is in the third person, as in "*She walked through flowers...*" (line 1), Lively uses *free indirect discourse* extensively to reveal Sandra's inner monologue. The story opens with the cottage already in sight, "*shrugged down into the dip*" (line 2) but it takes until line 69 for Sandra to reach the gate. In the interval, we hear mainly the thoughts in Sandra's head, time expanding to accommodate them. When Sandra is thinking, Lively uses her *idiolect* to express these thoughts, feelings and memories: "*They could have a good giggle, doing the floors and that.*" (line 15) or "*It was all right out here in the sunshine*" (line 35). This gives Sandra's experience an intimacy which makes it feel like it is written in the first person, but allows Lively to order the plot, describe the setting and other characters, and comment on them, outside of Sandra's limited perspective.

Setting

Lively describes the setting of the walk, the spinney and the cottage in colourful detail. She contrasts the light, airy countryside, full of flowers, through which Sandra walks, with the imagined darkness of the wood and the metaphorical darkness of the cottage. Setting is used to develop character, associating Sandra's innocence with sunshine and flowers, Kerry's hidden depths with his coming and going amongst the bushes, and Mrs Rutter's dark heart hidden beneath a cheery exterior and cute china ornaments.

Sandra walks in carefree innocence through fields of flowers where *"polleny summer grass that glinted in the sun"* (line 13) dusts her brown legs. She shuns the dark of the spinney, it being *"all right here in the sunshine"* (line 35). In the sunshine, she can daydream about her future, one that is hazy and does not extend beyond pictures in travel brochures, falling in love and having a sewing machine – all given equal importance.

The intrusion of *"Packers End"* on her daydreams and the shadow it casts on the day and on her thoughts, is conveyed by the use of the incomplete sentence *"Packer's End"*, placed deliberately at the end of the paragraph, where it *"shuts off the bare wide sky"* (line 23). To Sandra, Packer's End is a place of mystery, ugliness and darkness. It is a *"dark slab of trees"*, *"rank"* with *"whippy saplings and bramble and a gully"* full of discarded rubbish. Sandra's thoughts venture further to possible horrors – the remains of the dead aircraftmen. This leads her back to childhood fairy-tales and to more recent tales of abducted girls. Packer's End seems to be a place where childhood ends, foreshadowing Mrs Rutter's tale.

Packer's End holds no imagined horrors for Mrs Rutter. She knows the truth of it and from her we get a very different picture. She says she is *"lucky"* to be so close to the wood with the "*primroses and that*" (line 105-106) and the "*bluebells*" which she used to pick, "*Jugs and jugs of them, for the scent.*" (Line 213 – 215). This reversal of perception – Sandra the innocent seeing it as dangerous, and Mrs Rutter the witch seeing it as a pretty place - mirrors the moral inversion of Mrs Rutter, who justifies leaving a young man to die.

Just like the Gingerbread Cottage in "*Hansel and Gretel*", the cottage at the edge of the spinney appears inviting, if you do not look below the surface. The lino floor was once brightly coloured, but is now worn; there are pictures on the walls, but they are carelessly "*torn from magazines*" (line 89); the alcove of the fireplace is decorated with china ornaments, but like the pictures, they are stereotypical of a kind of store-bought sentimentalism – "*big-eyed*", "*beribboned*", "*flowery*" "*daisy chains*" (lines 90-91); the armchair sags; there are "*clumps of fluff*" in the cracks in the floorboards. The sulphurous "*smell of cabbage*" pervades the whole. The air of neglect and decay extends to the garden, which once had the potential for growth. It is now "*bedraggled*", with "*stumps of spent vegetables and a matted flower bed*" with "*shaggy grass*" (lines 102-103). The spinney reaches out towards the garden, as if trying to envelop it. The cottage and the garden tell of the corruption of Mrs Rutter's heart.

Lively contrasts the grim reality of the cottage and garden with Sandra's daydream of "*a little white house*" with a "*crisp green lawn*" (line 166-167), a fairy-tale cottage where she will play at being wife and mother, no doubt as she played with her dollhouse. By doing this, Lively causes the reader to reflect on whether this was Mrs Rutter's dream as well, before her husband was killed. Did grief at his loss turn a former "Sandra" into a witch?

Characterisation

Lively characterises through setting and through detailed description, often using metaphor, simile and symbolism.

Sandra's ignorance of the world is conveyed by Lively opening the story with a botanical list of the flowers the girl walks through *"ox-eye daisies, vetch and cow parsley"* and later by commenting that Sandra *"would pick a blue flower… and wonder what it was called"* (line 65). Sandra is portrayed as an innocent abroad, and of limited experience. When Lively writes, ironically, that her mother describes her as *"nervy"* (line 157), one might substitute *"spoiled and self-absorbed"*. She *"keeps to the track"* (line 2) of her own thoughts and stays on familiar territory, not venturing further afield and fearful of the unknown, which is described to her by others in scary stories. She forms her opinions on the words of others and makes judgements based on appearances. She describes Pat, the co-ordinator of the visits, disparagingly: *"Pat had a funny eye. Are all people who help other people not very nice-looking?"*. She admires Mrs Carpenter, who works in the local pub, for her superficial attractiveness, with her *"Platinum highlights and spike-heel suede boots"*. It is this judgement by appearances that leads her astray with Kerry Stevens, judging him by his *""black, licked-down hair and slitty eyes"* (line 75) and Mrs Rutter with her *"creamy, smiling pool of a face"* (line 85), her cute china ornaments and *"lovely…turquoise"* nightie (line 204).

Sandra is an adolescent on the verge of womanhood; she has an intense narcissistic interest in her own body: *"She looked down at her own legs"* (line 12); *"she looked at them [her bare toes], clean and plump and neat"* (line 37). Mrs Rutter is instinctively aware of this and uses it to try and create a shared intimacy between them, perhaps remembering, and reliving, her own youth. She causes Sandra to *"blush"* and become acutely aware of *"the soft skin of her thigh"* and that *"her breasts poke up and out."* (line

113). As yet, Sandra's ideas about men and sex are mere fantasies, where men are fairy-tale princes. In her fantasy, she sees herself with children in her own image first and men later: *"and ther'd be this man"* (line 169). She only sees Kerry as a man after the revelation: *"He had grown; he had grown older and larger"* (line 323).

As when describing the cottage, Lively juxtaposes positive with negative images to create a feeling that the *"creamy smiling pool of a face"* that is **Mrs Rutter** does indeed contain horrors beneath the surface. Like her cottage, Mrs Rutter is outwardly pleasant. *"Pat"* describes her as a *"dear old thing"* (line 4). She is like a *"cottage-loaf"*, a metaphor which initially seems homely and inviting, but Lively follows up with *"chins collapsed one into another"*, which suggests something soft, shapeless and rotting (line 85). Her eyes also tell of something hidden; they *"snapped and darted"*, *"glittered"*, *"investigated"* and *"examined"* suggesting calculation and weighing up, at odds with the soft exterior. The simile *"quick as mice"* (line 95-96) introduces the idea of this side of Mrs Rutter showing itself only momentarily, easily missed and quickly hidden again. As the tale progresses, these descriptions become more sinister; the *"chins shook, the pink and creamy chins"* (line 286) as she laughs at Sandra's squeamishness.

The difference between appearance and reality, between Sandra's innocence and Mrs Rutter's bitter experience, is symbolised by the flowered chocolate tin. Holding out the tin to Sandra, she says *"Look at the little cornflowers. And the daisies. They're almost real, aren't they?"* (line 160).

Mrs Rutter is vicariously[25] interested in Sandra; less so in Kerry. She is dismissive of Kerry, but perhaps also wary after she has *"examined him"*. She dismisses his aspiration to work in a garage

---

[25] Experiencing something indirectly through another.

as *"nothing special"* (line 101). She banishes him to the garden, to the *"shaggy grass"*, the compost heap and the wood kindling. She refers to him as *"what's-'is-name"* (line 162). Through Sandra, she appears to be reliving her youth, in her frequent references to Sandra being *"pretty"*, her references to Sandra's "boyfriends", her intimate reference to her showing a *"bit of bum"*, and her reminiscing on her wedding-dress when she finds that Sandra also makes dresses.

Mrs Rutter is also characterised by her constant talking. Mrs Rutter does not converse, listening and responding. It is her monologue and its effect on the boy and girl which creates much of the tension and leads to the devastating climax. Lively subtly characterises her monologue by reference to the chair from which she delivers it. The armchair is a *"composite chintzy mass from which cushions oozed and her voice flowed softly on"* (line 123-124). The words *"oozed"* suggests something sluggish and unwholesome, Mrs Rutter's words flowing sluggishly like a polluted stream. It is this monologue that tells the tragic tale of the crashed airman, never varying in emphasis, interspersed, even at moments of horror, with laughter when the *"chins shook, the pink and creamy chins."* (line 266). She delivers the revelation that she left the airman to die alone in the same neutral tone she discusses the weather: *"Went back inside. It was bucketing down, cats and dogs."* (line 279).

Lively contrasts this monotonal delivery with the increasingly horrified reaction of Kerry and Sandra, who grow increasingly "still": *"the boy stared at her"*; *"said the boy warily"*, *"the girl stiffened"*; *"there was silence"*, *"the boy and girl sat quite still"*; *"he did not move"* (line 257-295). The tension is broken when the realisation of the woman's callous action becomes unmistakable and the boy shoves back his chair. But even this does not stop the poisonous trickle. Even when Kerry gets up and declares he is leaving, Mrs Rutter continues to talk, in the same tone, about the everyday matters of which she makes herself the centre.

Kerry Stevens is, at first, an unlikely Prince in this tale. We see him initially through Sandra's eyes, her opinion of him based on others' opinions: *"Kerry Stevens that none of her lot reckoned much on."* (line 74-75). He is physically unattractive to her with his *"black, licked-down hair and slitty eyes"* (line 75) and *"his chin explosive with acne"*, his *"pale, chilly flesh"* (line 117). Sandra associates him with dirt – under his finger nails from gardening and from his aspiration to work in a garage with its *"oily workshop floors"* and *"fetid undersides of cars"* (line 179), when she cannot bear *"a stain or spot"* (line 186). She views him *"over a chasm"* (line 193), dismissing his wariness about Mrs Rutter as immaturity.

But Kerry is a Prince Charming. He has hidden depths which are symbolised by his coming and going amongst the bushes at Packer's End and in the cottage garden, half-seen, half-hidden: *"He rose …from beyond the hedge"* (line 69); *"she could see the bushes thrash and Kerry's head bob among them"* (line 154); *"he came up…"* (line 170). He waits for her as she walks towards the cottage, popping up from the hedge to mock-frighten her in a show of offered friendship; shares his chocolate with her; he remembers that he has worked on her Dad's car. Mrs Rutter describes him as *"a nice boy"* but aligns herself with Sandra in commenting on his use of hair-gel. She is also, perhaps, wary of him, recognising a potentially more critical audience. Kerry is clear-sighted and empathetic, rooted in the real world of jobs to be done and work to be had in the future. His is not a fantasy world, but one based on his own reason and experience. He acts decisively in declaring he is leaving, rescuing Sandra from her paralysis. His reaction to Mrs Rutter's tale is explosive and instinctive: *"Christ!"* and *"Two bloody nights. Christ!"* (lines 311 and 319).

Themes, Symbolism and Imagery

Rather than a single, main symbol being used to underpin the theme, symbolism and imagery are woven throughout the Tale, in the setting, and characterisation.

This is a tale about **things hidden** and **the deceptiveness of appearances**. The title *"The Darkness Out There"* establishes the theme of a *"world grown unreliable"*, as Sandra sees it when reality intrudes on her childish fantasies, but conceals that the darkness of the story lies within the dark heart of Mrs Rutter – the darkness **in** there.

It is also a **coming-of-age** story, or story of **innocence and experience**. Sandra is presented at the beginning as an innocent, associated with flowers and sunlight. As the story progresses, the shadow of what happened in the spinney intrudes onto her life, darkening her fantasy world and forcing her to re-evaluate all she has ever known. She has to leave behind the fairy-tales of witches and wolves, and *"gypsy-type blokes"* (line 313). Sandra is forced to grow-up and confront the darkness in the real world: *"One moment you were walking in long grass…and the next you glimpsed…inescapable darkness"* (line 329).

Links

The theme of "coming-of-age" is shared with all the stories in the anthology, with the exception of *"Odour of Chrysanthemums"* and *"My Polish Teacher's Tie"*.

"Korea", *"A Family Supper"* and *"Chemistry"* all have themes of things hidden below the surface or appearance versus reality.

"Korea" and *"Odour of Chrysanthemums"* explore the difficulties of truly knowing another person and the deceptiveness of appearance.

Printed in Great Britain
by Amazon